THE GOLDEN DROPLET

(La Goutte d'Or)

MICHEL TOURNIER

The Golden Droplet

La Goutte d'Or
*Translated from the French
by Barbara Wright*

Doubleday
NEW YORK
1987

Library of Congress Cataloging in Publication Data

Tournier, Michael.
The golden droplet.

Translation of: La goutte d'or.
I. Title.
PQ2680.083G613 1987   843'.914
ISBN 0-385-23759-6
Library of Congress Catalog Card Number: 87-8881
First Published as *La Goutte d'Or* by Éditions Gallimard, Paris
© 1985 Éditions Gallimard
English Translation © 1987 by Doubleday & Company, Inc.,
& William Collins Sons & Company, Limited
All Rights Reserved
Printed in the United States of America
First Edition in the United States of America

You are so exactly what you seem that I can't hear what you say.

THOMAS JEFFERSON

THE GOLDEN DROPLET

(La Goutte d'Or)

One

THE FLYING SQUAD OF GOATS, always intent on scattering into the scree, was induced back to the serried, docile mass of the sheep by a volley of stones. Idris drove his little flock farther toward the reddening line of the dunes than he had done on either of the two previous days. The week before, having promised to do the same for them sometime, he had persuaded Baba and Mabruk to accompany him, and the days had passed like a dream. But his two friends had since been confined to the garden to help their father clear the sand out of his irrigation channels. At fifteen, Idris was no longer of an age to admit that his dread of solitude lent wings to his legs and prevented him from settling down comfortably in the shade of a wild arbutus to wait for the time to pass, as he had done with his friends. He knew, no doubt, that the winds blowing from the confines of the desert are not jinns who carry off scatter-brained, disobedient children, as his grandmother had told him, according to an oral tradition that no doubt dated back to the days when the nomads used to make forays on the peasant populations of the oases. But this legend had left its traces in his heart, and the deceptive shimmering of the first sunbeams on the Chott el Ksob, the desperate retreat of a big monitor lizard disturbed in its bed of sand by his naked feet, the pale flight of an owl bewildered by the early morning light, all impelled him to seek some human contact without delay. In driving his flock eastward, his idea was to join Ibrahim ben Larbi, one of the shepherds of the semi-nomadic Chaamba tribes who camp along the Er-raoui erg and are the professional custodians of the oasis camels, for which service they receive all their milk and half of their increase in stock.

Idris knew that he wouldn't find his friend in his community, whose low black tents occupied a zone containing an abundance of wells, the Oglat Melouane, most of which, it is true, had caved in, but which nevertheless sufficed for human needs. In fact, the animals grazed within a radius of some twenty kilometers, each herd containing a dozen adult camels and as many colts, and each guarded by a boy who had his own accredited well. Idris made his way more to the north, in the direction of the rocky defile beyond which Ibrahim's domain began. This was an arid reg, sparsely strewn with clumps of saltwort and euphorbia, where the east wind had left long trails of delicately sculptured, tawny sand. He no longer had to goad the animals to keep them moving. From there on, the proximity of Ibrahim's well, the Hassi Ourit, acted like an invisible magnet on the sheep and they quickened their pace, closely followed by the goats. It was still not possible to see anything other than the tormented outlines of the rare stumps of dead trees, or the gentle slopes dotted with abesquis which the young goats would jump up and perch on. But on the gray cliff of the erg, Idris was soon able to make out the parasol-shaped outline of the acacia shading the well. He was still two kilometers away when he came across a she-camel kneeling on the gravel and obviously in a bad way. He got her to her feet, she groaned plaintively, and set off at a limping trot in front of the flock. Idris was not displeased to be appearing to the Chaamba bringing him back an animal he had perhaps lost.

The relations between the two adolescents were simple and unequivocal: on Idris's part a somewhat timid admiration, on Ibrahim's a protective and condescending friendship. Because he was a nomad, left to his own devices, and a cameleer, Ibrahim's attitude toward the oasis dwellers was one of indulgent scorn, in no way tempered by the fact that he worked for them and owed them his livelihood. In this attitude there was a kind of reminiscence of a glorious past in which the oases and the slaves who cultivated them were the indiscriminate property of the nomadic seigneurs. For all that, this boy, whom sun and solitude had made a little mad, feared neither god nor devil, and knew how to turn even the aridity of the desert to account. Ibrahim's single eye, the left one—his right eye had remained stuck in the thorns of a gum-tree wood into which his camel had precipitated itself—could distinguish from a distance of two kilometers the flight of a gazelle or the tribe to which a donkey-boy belonged. His tough, lean legs could carry him twenty-four hours at a stretch with neither water nor dates. He could find his bearings without the slightest deviation at night or in a sandstorm. And in any case, he knew how to make the wind veer by impaling a sacred scarab on a needle and orienting in the desired direction the irresistible movement of its legs as they paddled in the void. By watching the path of an ant he could find the anthill, kick it to bits, and thus obtain a succulent meal by winnowing the contents of its galleries, even though these insects were greatly feared in Tabelbala because their subterranean residence brings them into contact with the jinns. His impiety often terrified Idris. He had no hesitation in drinking standing up, holding his bowl in a single hand, whereas when one drinks one must have at least one knee on the ground, and clasp the bowl in both hands. He spoke openly about fire, thus recklessly invoking hell, whereas the oasis dwellers prudently use expressions such as "the little old man that crackles" or "the thing that makes ashes." He wasn't even afraid of putting out a fire by throwing water on it, which is profanatory. One day Idris had seen him feasting on a sheep's brain, a morsel that in Tabelbala is always buried, because anyone who eats it is driven mad just as surely as if he were to devour his own brain.

When he got to the shade of the acacia, still preceded by the limping she-camel, Idris didn't find Ibrahim there. His animals jostled one another around the small circular basin, fed from the overflow of the well, where a residue of sandy water was stagnating. They could have managed without a drink until the evening, but the basin was a useful center of attraction that prevented them from dispersing.

Where was Ibrahim? Had he perhaps taken his camels to a remote pasture created in just a few hours by a storm? Idris looked for traces of him around the tree, but the ground was riddled with prints in which the large soles of the camels were mixed up with the small holes made by the hooves of the goats and sheep. He then walked around in a circle a short distance away from the well, trying to find some indication of the direction the Chaamba had taken. He spotted the irregular trail left by a monitor lizard, the tiny stars that betrayed the jumping action of a jerboa, the triangular and rather old trace of a fennec at the gallop. He walked around a lump of basalt whose blackness made a strong contrast with the reg, which was becoming more and more dazzling as the sun climbed up the horizon. And then he discovered some prints of such enormous interest that his mind immediately became a blank. He forgot all about Ibrahim and his camels, and even about his own herd. The only things that existed were the two finely serrated ribbons which had carved out shallow grooves in the white ground and were visible as far as the eye could see. A car, an automobile, a thing no one in the oasis had ever spoken about, had suddenly loomed up out of the darkness with its cargo of material riches and human mystery! Choking with excitement, Idris dashed off in pursuit of the vehicle, which was disappearing westward.

The sun was blazing high in the sky when he saw, in the quivering, overheated ground, gliding along by a tamarisk copse, the clumsy contours of a Land-Rover. It wasn't traveling very fast, but Idris hadn't the slightest chance of catching up with it. Nor did he even dream of doing so. He stopped, immobilized by astonishment and timidity, and was soon surrounded by his sheep and goats. The Land-Rover, turning northward, was now starting along the track leading to Beni-Abbès. In five minutes it would be out of sight. No. It slowed down. It made a U-turn. It gathered speed and began to charge at him. There were two people in it, a man at the wheel and, sitting beside him, a woman; at first Idris could see nothing of her but her blonde hair and big sunglasses. The car stopped. The woman took off her glasses and jumped out. Her bleached hair hung down over her shoulders. She was wearing a very low-cut khaki top and a pair of outrageously abbreviated shorts. Idris also noticed her golden ballet slippers and thought that she wouldn't go far with them in the surrounding gravel. She was brandishing a camera.

"Hey, boy! Don't move too much, I'm going to photograph you."

"You might at least ask his opinion," the man muttered. "Some of these people don't like it."

"You're a fine one to say that!" the woman remarked.

Idris listened carefully and mustered up the oddments of French he possessed to try to understand what they were saying. It was obvious that he was the subject of an argument between the man and the woman, but that it was the woman who was interested in him, and this was what disturbed him the most.

"Don't delude yourself," said the man derisively, "he's much more interested in the car than he is in you!"

It was true that the car was impressive; squat, white with dust, bristling with cans, spare wheels, jacks, fire extinguishers, towropes, shovels, perforated metal sheets for freeing it from the sand. As a connoisseur of the desert, Idris admired this long-distance cruising vehicle which was not without some re-

[5]

mote affinity with a sumpter camel. Men who possessed such prestigious implements could only be seigneurs.

"I'm not deluding myself," said the woman, "but I don't think he sees any difference. The car and us—it's the same foreign world. Both you and I are emanations of the Land-Rover."

She had wound her camera several times and was once again focusing it on Idris and his sheep. She was smiling now as she looked at him, and without her camera she finally seemed to be seeing him normally.

"Give me the photo."

These were the first words that Idris uttered.

"He wants his photo; only natural, isn't it?" the man put in. "We should always bring a Polaroid camera, you know. The poor kid will be disappointed."

The woman had put the camera back in the car. She brought out a map covered with cellophane. She went up to Idris.

"I can't possibly, young man. I have to get the film developed and printed. We'll send you your photo. Look. This is where we are, see? Tabelbala. The green patch is your oasis. Tomorrow Beni-Abbès. Then Béchar. Then Oran. There, the car ferry. Twenty-five hours on the sea. Marseille. Eight hundred kilometers on the autoroute. Paris. And from there, we'll send you your photo. What's your name?"

After the Land-Rover had disappeared, raising a cloud of dust, Idris was no longer quite the same man. There was only one photograph in Tabelbala. In the first place because the oasis dwellers are too poor to bother about photography. And next because the image is feared by these Muslim Berbers. They attribute a maleficent power to it; they believe that it in some way materializes the evil eye. And yet this unique photo contributed to the prestige of Lance Sergeant Mogadem ben Abderrahman, Idris's uncle, who had returned from the Italian campaign with a mention in dispatches and the Croix de Guerre. Mention, Croix de Guerre, and photo were all displayed on the wall of his gourbi, and in the cracked and rather fuzzy image he could be seen, bursting with youth and high spirits, in the company of two facetious-looking comrades. Up till then there had been only one photo in Tabelbala, thought Idris; from now on there will be another—mine.

He scurried along the white reg in the direction of the tall acacia tree at Hassi Ourit. He was bubbling over with the adventure he had just lived through and was already anticipating the pleasure of boasting about it to Ibrahim. Really boasting about it? What proof did he have? If only they had given him his photo! No, though, his image was now on its way to Beni-Abbès, shut inside the camera case, which itself was tucked away in the Land-Rover. The car too was fast becoming unreal, the farther away he got. He would soon be out of sight of its tire tracks. Any minute now there would be nothing to prove the reality of his recent encounter.

When he got to Ourit, Ibrahim greeted him as usual with a hail of stones. This too was something that oasis dwellers would never have done to each other. Picking up a stone is already a hostile gesture, although it is a threat that you are fortunately still a long way from carrying out. Ibrahim enjoyed the diabolical skill in stone throwing that he had acquired from his earliest childhood. He could unerringly hit a crow in full flight, a fennec at full gallop. For the moment, seeing his friend approach, as a welcoming gesture he was playing at making the sand spray up to his right, to his left, in front of him, and even between his feet, less in the hope of frightening him—Idris had long known that he was in no danger—than simply to manifest his pleasure at seeing him in a way that combined his aggressiveness with his natural gifts. He stopped when the distance between them had become too short for the game to present any further interest.

"Come here!" he cried. "I've got some news for you!"

There! That was Ibrahim all over! Idris had had an unheard-of experience. He had undergone the ordeal of photography, and by a blonde woman what was more, he had unexpectedly become someone comparable to Lance Sergeant Mogadem,

[7]

and a couple of hours later it was Ibrahim who had news for him!

"One of my she-camels is going to drop her colt at the Hassi el Hora well. It's an hour from here. The well is rotten, but she has to drink. We must go there with some milk."

He pronounced the Berber language in staccato phrases which sounded like so many imperative barks. At the same time, his single eye was sparkling with irony, because Idris was only a foolish oasis dweller, a "round tail," docile, gentle, but no match for a Chaamba cameleer. An old male camel braced itself and spurted a stream of urine onto the sand. Ibrahim took advantage of this to rinse his hands, because a Chaamba doesn't milk with dirty hands. Then he swung a she-camel around, to get her into the right position for milking, and started to untie the net imprisoning her teats to protect them from the colts in the herd. Finally he began to milk, standing on one leg, his left foot resting on his right knee, with a clay bowl balanced on his left thigh.

Idris watched the two jets squirting alternately into the bowl. In a permanent state of undernourishment, he suffered from the desire aroused in him by this white, warm, living liquid that would have been capable of appeasing both his hunger and his thirst. The camel flapped her little bear's ears and, opening her anus, released a flood of green diarrhea onto the insides of her thighs, manifestations of the confidence and abandon induced by the flow of her milk.

Ibrahim stopped milking when he judged that he had enough milk to fill one of the dried gourds which are given a lid and hung from the camel's flank in a netting made of palm fibers. He went up to the old male and, without having to touch it, with a simple guttural cry made it kneel. Then he perched himself on its neck, his back leaning against its hump, and got Idris to sit in front of him. The camel stood up with an angry roar and immediately darted off toward the north. After crossing a zone of reddish earth strewn with the occasional treelike shrub, they entered the bed of a wadi and went up it for several kilometers. Carved out by the water—water which had obviously not flowed for several years—the ground consisted of vast, smooth, sunbaked patches which cracked violently under the broad feet of the camel. Several times the two riders were nearly thrown to the ground. The animal snarled with fury. They had to slow down. The camel came to a complete halt at the foot of a basalt rock under which it had scented the presence of a guelta. Ibrahim let it drink the gray water on which insects were zigzagging. It raised its sad, haughty head, dilated its dripping nostrils, and let out a roar that smelled of salt and sulfur. Then it began to run again. As they came closer to Hassi el Hora, Idris could feel his companion's growing anxiety and impatience. There was misfortune in the air, as his unerring instinct warned the Chaamba.

The only sign of the presence of a well was a slight acclivity —the very old and hardened remains of the dug-out earth. Neither basin, nor curb, nor rim; it was merely a dangerously open round hole, flush with the ground. However, a flimsy hut of intertwined poles and palm branches showed that the shepherds knew this water hole and sometimes rested by it, protected from the sun, after watering their animals. For the time being it was deserted. But from a very long way away Ibrahim's one eye made out the spindly beige silhouette of a newborn camel colt, abandoned between the well and the shelter. His worst forebodings were confirmed.

He jumped down from the camel and ran straight to the edge of the well. Idris saw him climb down onto the most accessible beam of the inner framework supporting the earthen walls, and lie down on it to get a better look at the bottom of the hole. There was no possible doubt. Thirsty after her parturition, the she-camel had gone up to the edge of the well and toppled over into the void. At this moment the colt uttered a plaintive cry and its mother answered it: from the depths of the well came a groan amplified as if by a gigantic organ pipe. Idris too leaned over the opening. At first all he could see was the crisscross of the beams keeping the coffering of the walls in place. But when his eyes had grown accustomed to the darkness, he could make out luminous, glistening reflections, a black silhouette lying on its flank, half submerged, and, like a tiny pinprick at the edge of this sinister picture, the image of his own outstretched, living head against the deep azure of the sky.

Ibrahim had got out of the well and was running over to the hut. He came back with a twisted-leather rope.

"I'm going down to see whether the camel's injured," he said. "If not, we'll get the other shepherds to help us try and pull her out. If she's broken a leg, we shall have to kill her."

Then, having tied one end of the rope around the top of a projecting rock, he gently lowered himself into the well. There was a silence. But his voice soon came up in cavernous echoes.

"She's got a broken leg. I'm going to slit her throat and cut her up. You can bring up the pieces. Start with my clothes."

Idris pulled up a light bundle of rags. Then he waited, without trying to see the horrible job the Chaamba was doing in the muddy water twenty meters belowground.

The big camel had gone up to the colt. He sniffed at it for a long time and then began to lick it tenderly. Idris observed the scene with amusement. It was hardly likely that the old male would have succumbed to a sudden paternal vocation. More probably, he was appreciating the pungent smell of the mother on the trembling, humid body of the baby. As for the colt, desperate with solitude, it huddled up to this unexpected protector and then, driven by instinct, stuck its muzzle up into his genitals, searching for hypothetical teats.

An imperious call roused Idris from his contemplation. He began to haul the heavily weighted rope. Soon he was pulling up a thigh and a leg, still warm with life. He took this piece of meat over to the shade of the hut. The cameleer's voice immediately rang out again.

"Draw a bucket of water, mix it with the milk we brought, and give the baby a drink."

So even in the thick of the exhausting job he was doing, Ibrahim hadn't forgotten the colt, and was sacrificing to it the only nourishment he had at his disposal. Idris obeyed reluctantly, but without envisaging the possibility of disobeying, by drinking some of the milk, for instance. He was subjugated by the superhuman courage of his friend. The colt was incapable of drinking. Idris had to improvise a baby's bottle for it by breaking the bottom of an ordinary bottle and turning it into a kind of funnel. He had only just begun to feed the colt in this way when a new quarter from the she-camel was sent up from the bottom of the well. When the sun had reached its highest point, he heard Ibrahim congratulating himself on the direct light it was giving him. The cabin was now no more than an accumulation of quarters of meat over which swarms of bluebottles buzzed furiously the moment they were disturbed. But what particularly worried Idris was that the sky, which had been clear only an hour before, was now filled with slowly drifting little black crosses which for a moment seemed motionless but then suddenly began to hover. The vultures had seen everything and were getting ready to dive. Even so, they were less to be feared than the crows, whose audacity and aggressiveness stopped at nothing. He imagined what their return journey would be like, with the colt barely able to walk, the big male balancing a pyramid of fresh meat on its hump, and the black, screeching trail of crows that would follow them.

He was surprised to see Ibrahim suddenly hauling himself up onto the crossbeam of the well. He was nothing but a living statue sculptured in bloodstained clay. Dazzled by the strong light, he covered his face with his hands and raised his head up to the sky. Then his hands slipped, and Idris saw that a clot of blood had become lodged in his hollow orbit, as if his eye had just been put out. The Chaamba was intoxicated with tension, fatigue, and midday exaltation. He raised his arms and let out a howl of triumph and defiance. Then he began to jump up and down, balancing on the beam. He had taken his penis in his hand and was holding it out toward Idris.

"Oh, round tail! Look! *My* tail is pointed!"

Once again he jumped on the worm-eaten beam. There was a crack, and the Chaamba disappeared as if down a trapdoor. A second crack told Idris that his friend's body had hit the main beam and that that too had given way. Then there was something like an earthquake. The ground moved. The cabin collapsed onto the quarters of the she-camel. A cloud of dust shot up into the sky from the well, and in its midst Idris could make out the panic-stricken flight of innumerable bats that spent the day in the framework of the well. The breaking of the two beams had led to the collapse of the whole coffering supporting the walls. The well had suddenly been filled in. Up to what level? Where was Ibrahim?

Idris went over to it. Less than two meters down, he could see sand mixed with broken bits of wood. He called his friend. His ineffectual voice sounded in a silence made still more sepulchral by the supremacy of the sun at its full zenith. Then he was seized with panic. He howled with fear and ran straight in front of him. He ran for a long time. Until he tripped over a tree stump and collapsed on the sand, shaken with sobs. But he got up at once, clasping his hands over his ears. Pressing his cheek to the ground, he thought he could hear, rising from the depths, the laughter of his friend . . . who had been buried alive.

Two

"HE PHOTOGRAPHED YOU? Where is it then, your photo?"

His mother was once again going over the story of the photo, while a matron, their neighbor Kuka, was helping her with her hair and makeup. He hadn't been able to keep to himself his encounter with the French couple in the Land-Rover and their promise to him: his photo. They were going to send it to him. It would arrive with the rare mail that came to the oasis with the supplies of food, tools, and clothes ordered each week and delivered by Salah Brahim, the carrier who provided the liaison with the big neighboring oasis, Beni-Abbès. But to humor his mother, who was always inclined to imagine the worst, he had said nothing about the role or even the existence of the blonde woman. There were only two men in the car, he had said, one of whom had taken the photo.

"It'll never come," Kuka ben Laïd prophesied darkly, unravelling his mother's hair with three iron spikes. "And then what? What are they going to do with that photo? No one can know!"

"It's a bit of yourself that's gone," his mother added. "If after that you get ill, how shall we be able to cure you?"

"It may well make him leave too," Kuka went on. "Three young men from the village who've emigrated north within six months!"

Idris was absorbed in some precision work. He was carving a little camel out of a lump of ocher-colored kaolin, and all the more carefully in that he wanted to be sure not to take any part in the morose litany of the two women. He had used his herd of sculptured camels since his earliest infancy for playing at being a Chaamba nomad. In the beginning, he had been given these pieces one by one. Later, he had painted his herd, and covered it with bits of material and palm fibers. Every day he watered it and led it out to pasture, and nursed the sick or injured animals. When he got too big for such childish pursuits, he gave them one by one to his younger brothers and carved new pieces that enriched an already numerous camel population.

"*I* know why these young people leave," said Kuka mysteriously.

There was a polite silence, and then the mother asked:

"Well? Why do these young people leave?"

"It's because they were taught to walk too early. It's a nomad taint that marks them for the rest of their lives."

"Idris didn't walk till he was two," said the mother, with some restraint.

She was hurt by the reminder of a family characteristic that had formerly tormented her with anxieties and somber presentiments: almost all her children had been late in walking. For her third, when he had reached the age of two, they had even organized the kind of rogation ceremony traditional in such cases. The child, dressed in rags and deliberately left snotty and soiled, was carried in a basket by two little girls—sisters, cousins, or failing these, neighbors—who went round to every house, chanting continuously during the whole of their round: "He doesn't walk, he won't walk, may God let him walk!"

Every family they visited made them a gift—wheat, barley, sugar, an onion, a small coin—which went into the basket, where it came in contact with the child. After that, the mother had to organize a little feast for the child who didn't walk and for the little girls who had walked in his place, for which they used the offerings brought back.

"Yes, but by the time he was six," Kuka insisted, "he was playing with a truck made out of a petrol can fitted with four clay wheels and one spare one. What did that mean?"

"If Idris is destined to leave, he will leave," the mother concluded fatalistically.

"Of course, but not necessarily under the evil eye," Kuka conceded, smearing the mother's hair with a thick unguent composed of henna, cloves, dried roses, and myrtle, which gave her coiffure a flattering fullness.

She had just pronounced the words that had been continually haunting the mother ever since she had heard about the Land-Rover episode. To avoid being injured by the evil eye, it is a wise precaution to make yourself as inconspicuous as possible. To attract the eye by your attire, your strength, or your beauty is to tempt the devil. Mothers in Tabelbala deliberately neglected their babies and left them fairly dirty to make sure that they didn't excite any admiration at a particularly vulnerable age. The man who proudly exhibits the brand-new knife he has just acquired is more likely than not to cut himself the first time he uses it. The nursing mother flaunting her ample breasts, the ostentatiously fecund she-goat, the abundantly flowering palm tree, all expose themselves to the gaze of the eye whose power desiccates, sterilizes, withers. What can be said, then, of the photographic eye, and of the imprudence of anyone who obligingly offers himself up to it!

Idris knew all this. He was sufficiently imbued with the Belbali spirit to tremble at the risks he deliberately exposed himself to. But at the same time he had a passionate desire to free himself from the influence of the oasis in which he had grown up. His admiration for the Chaamba nomads led him in this direction, as did the little herd of carved camels that he still cherished at an age when one made oneself ridiculous by indulging in such childish pursuits. His mother didn't think much of this collection, of course, but Idris was a boy, he would soon be a man, and camels after all were not dolls, playthings she would not even have tolerated in the hands of her daughters.

Kuka had carefully made a ball out of the hair that had remained in the comb. It was important that not a single one should go astray; being a personal emanation of the mother, each one retained a direct influence on her physical and mental health. If these hairs were to fall into malevolent hands they would constitute a dangerous instrument for casting spells. Yet there could be no question of burning them. They would be buried at the foot of a tamarisk, a tree that is the object of a feminine cult.

"Is it true that Idris was sold to the blacks?" Kuka suddenly asked.

It was a tactless question, and the matron would no doubt not have had the nerve to ask it in front of a witness, or even face to face. But as the mother had her back to her and was abandoning herself to Kuka's hands, she could elude it without too much vehemence, or even oppose it with silence.

"Yes," she said, after some thought. "Before he was born I had two stillborn children."

This was sufficient explanation. When fate is hounding a family, on the day a child is born they call upon the services of the little community of the descendants of Negro slaves at the oasis. They come and dance in front of the house. The father symbolically places the baby on the chief's drum, and gives the community a sizable present both in cash and in kind. If the child lives, the Negroes, who have thus taken his destiny in hand, will have the right to a new donation, but he himself will have to remember his protectors for the rest of his life. Until he was six, Idris had had his hair done traditionally like that of the Negro children, his head completely shaven with the exception of a thick tuft starting from his forehead and running over his head like a crest to the back of his neck.

Kuka didn't insist, but the mother understood that she saw in this detail one more reason why Idris would leave his family. She was patiently braiding—taking care not to draw the hair too tightly together, for this may cause sterility—the three customary plaits of married women: two rather thin lateral ones decorated with silver rings and one thick dorsal one that passed through a cone shell symbolizing a protecting eye.

The matron was now about to start painting the mother's face, and she changed her position and went and squatted down in front of her. This was the signal for Kuka's part in the conversation to take on a less insidious turn, and for the mother's to become more frankly reticent. Idris managed to get himself forgotten, as he had learned to do every time when, in the tiny dwelling, he was present at a scene from which he was theoretically excluded on account of his age or sex. But he was thinking about the celebrations which were to begin that evening and continue for ten days: Ahmed ben Baada was marrying his daughter Ayesha to Mohammed ben Souhil's eldest son, and a troupe of dancers and musicians from the High Atlas Mountains was coming to lend its color and rhythms to the ceremonies.

Three

THROUGHOUT THE DAY the women in the future bride-groom's house had been preparing a tazou that would be enough for a hundred and fifty to two hundred people. For three hours a dozen matrons had been working with their limestone grinders to manufacture the necessary semolina. The excitement sustained by this continuously talking, singing, clucking chorus was communicated to the interested spectators filing past to see the display of the presents given by the young man's family to that of the future bride. They appraised the pieces of cloth, the scarves, belts, slippers, silver bracelets and necklaces, combs, mirrors, eau de cologne, and those products without which no feminine beauty can exist: henna, myrtle, incense, walnut bark, cloves, and wild iris rhizomes. In the extreme poverty of the oasis, such a display constituted a feast for the eyes that no one could miss.

In the afternoon a modest, almost timid dance brought the women together. Couples were formed between married women and girls, as if the girls were to receive an initiation from their elders. The fiancé, for his part, accompanied by his "viziers"—seven or eight celibate friends—came back from a somewhat mysterious wood-gathering expedition, vouched for by the half dozen donkeys laden with bundles of firewood which they were driving in front of them. Custom demands that the bridegroom should be enveloped up to the eyes in a vast burnous girdled by the rope that helped his mother bring him into the world. The truth is that he will have spent the night carousing with his habitual companions, to mark the end of his adolescence. In this way the segregation of the sexes is doubly celebrated on the eve of a marriage.

Idris only participated in these rites to the degree with which he managed to identify himself with the fiancé—who was only three years older than he—but it was a very limited degree. Ibrahim's tragic death had opened up a great gulf of friendship around him which no oasis boy had been able to fill. The bride was of his own age. They had grown up together, and this fat, flabby, passive girl had neither mystery nor prestige in his eyes. It was quite likely that she had no more of either in those of her future husband. But Ali ben Mohammed remained faithful to the tradition according to which husband and wife love and respect one another because they have been united by the marriage ceremony; their feelings are supposed to be the effect and not the cause of their union. The opposite idea, however—that love comes first and is the most important reason for marriage—this modern, impious idea, had insidiously obtruded itself into Idris's mind. Since the bride was seen as holding no charm, the whole celebration seemed to him an unnecessary encumbrance, and even in a way a virtual menace to his freedom, although he was determined to thwart all the maneuvers of his mother and of the parents of any nubile oasis girl aiming to embark him upon the matrimonial path. At the sight of this young man solemnly putting down his roots in Tabelbala by becoming a husband, and soon no doubt also a father, Idris felt his heels growing wings, and he thought longingly, fervently, about the blonde photographer who had taken his image from him and carried it away with her in her dream vehicle. Two contradictory scenes, actually, were fighting for possession of his imagination. One day, Salah Brahim, jumping down from his truck, was giving him an envelope posted in Paris in which he found his photograph. But more often he saw himself taking the road northward on a long march which would end in Paris. Old Kuka had guessed correctly; his only thought was to leave.

Night had long fallen when a tumult coming from the Chraïa ksar brought the guests out of their houses. The lime-washed walls of the gourbis, aglow with the projected lights of the flambeaux, looked as if they were on fire. Raucous cries and high-pitched youyous, the muffled boom of drumrolls and the strident sounds of trumpets rent the nocturnal silence. It was the troupe of mountain dwellers who had come from the west by way of the Hammada du Drâa and who were serenading the young couple in their own fashion. The drums were letting all hell loose. Each instrument was carried horizontally, tied around the player's waist, and was capable of two sounds, one clear and one muffled, according to whether one of its extremities was beaten with a stick or the other with a fist. The nasal whine of the bagpipes provided a ground bass above which two soloists blowing into short copper trumpets took turns tracing the curve of an obsessive ritornello. This was far removed from the pure, limpid monologue that Idris sometimes produced, at the hottest hours of the day, from his six-holed reed pipe.

The players had formed a semicircle, brightly and capriciously illuminated by the flambeaux, in front of Mohammed ben Souhil's house. The music became more impassioned, louder and louder, and communicated an uncontrollable frenzy to the motionless bodies of the spectators. The rhythm increased in intensity, with the aim, as everyone could see, of engendering the dance, of metamorphosing the entire group of musicians into one single dance. And the birth took place: a black woman, dressed in red veils and silver jewelry, suddenly appeared in the center of the open space. Zett Zobeida never showed herself until the celebrations were at their height, for she was their soul and their flame. First, with her body bent forward, she ran with rapid steps to the edge of the circle that belonged to her, as if to take possession of her domain. Then she described a series of more and more concentrated figures. It was clear: she was gleaning all the music spread over her area, gathering up, like an invisible harvest, all the dance scattered around her. From then on the crowd danced with her, and everyone repeated a haunting, enigmatic litany:

> *The dragonfly flutters low over the water*
> *The cricket creaks on the stone*
> *The dragonfly flutters and wordlessly twitters*
> *The cricket creaks and utters no word*
> *But the dragonfly's wing is a skit*
> *But the cricket's wing is a script*
> *And this skit thwarts the tricks of death*
> *And this script tells the secret of life.*

Zett Zobeida was now dancing with very tiny steps, closely encircled by the musicians. Soon her feet were moving on the spot, for the entire dance had entered her body. And all that could be seen of this body, between the bottom of her corsage and the top of her skirt, was a hand of shining black nudity. In the middle of this veiled statue, all that was dancing was her belly, animated by an autonomous and intensely expressive life. This belly was the lipless mouth of her entire body, the speaking, smiling, grimacing, singing part of the entire body:

> *The dragonfly phrases the tricks of death*
> *The cricket writes the secret of life.*

Zett Zobeida's dance had now become the ballet of a hundred sonorous jewels on this immobile, veiled statue. Hands of Fatma and crescent moons, gazelles' hooves and mother-of-pearl shells, coral necklaces and amber bracelets, amulets, stars, and pomegranate-shaped gems performed their dance in a great clinking confabulation. But Idris's gaze was particularly attracted by a jewel twisting around on a leather thong—a golden droplet of admirable shape and brilliance. It was impossible to conceive of an object of a simpler and more compact perfection. Everything seemed to be contained in that oval, slightly swollen at its base. Everything seemed to be expressed in the silence of that solitary bubble which didn't come into contact with any other jewel in its brief oscillations. Unlike those crystal pendants that imitate the sky, the earth, the animals of the desert and the fish of the sea, the golden bubble had no other meaning than itself. It was pure sign, absolute form.

That evening Idris might well have begun to suspect that Zett Zobeida and her golden droplet were the emanation of a world without images, the antithesis of, and perhaps the antidote to, the platinized woman with the camera. He might well have progressed further into his initiation if, after the songs and dances, in the restored calm of the scintillating night, Abdullah Fehr, the black storyteller from the borders of the Sudan and the Tibesti Mountains, had not told them the adventure of the former pirate Khair ed-Din, who for a short time had become king of Tunis and who had encountered so many difficulties because of his hair and beard.

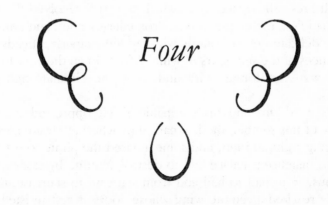

Four

Barbarossa; or, The King's Portrait

HIS REAL NAME was Khair ed-Din, but the Roumis, out of derision, called him Barbarossa. This former Levantine pirate had buccaneered over the whole of the Mediterranean with his older brother. Together they had made themselves masters of Algiers, whose port they had fortified to shelter their forty galleys. Then the older brother was killed in Tlemcen, and the younger pursued a brilliant career on his own. In the year 912[1] of the Hegira, he captured Bizerte and drove the Sultan of Tunis, Moulay Hassan, out of his Bardo palace.

When Khair ed-Din and his companions, still reeking with the blood of battle, irrupted into the interior of the palace, they were struck by the silence that suddenly surrounded them, and they had the strange feeling that they had entered an enchanted realm. There was no sign of life on the patios, on the succession of terraces, in the enormous halls, under the colonnades festooning the dreamlike gardens. The proud, noble residence, so it seemed, had only the moment before been deserted by its courtiers, soldiers, servants, and guards, and

---

[1] 1534 of the Christian era.

delivered up intact to the seafaring barbarians, with its balda-
chins, its screens, its cushions, its china, and even its hearths in
which fires still burned, over which spits still revolved. Everyone had fled, taking the horses, dromedaries, apes, and salukis,
those delicate desert hounds who lay their tapering heads on
the knees of the seigneurs of white Africa. Even the very foun-
tains were no longer surrounded by the circular flight of
doves.

Khair ed-Din and his companions felt oppressed by the
magic of this somber abode. Fearing treachery, they advanced,
glancing right and left, and some advised the pirate to set fire
to this maleficent palace and to destroy it stone by stone.

Thus, from hall to hall and from staircase to staircase, they
finally reached a remote wing whose doors at first resisted all
their efforts. They had to decide to break one down, and this
the soldiers had begun to do when it opened of its own accord.
A tall, severe-looking man, dressed in a white robe bedaubed
with multicolored blotches, appeared, looking surprised and
wrathful.

"What is the meaning of all this commotion?" he said. "I
gave strict orders that I was not to be disturbed in my work!"

An Ottoman guard, armed with a scimitar, advanced with
the obvious intention of severing the head of the man who
dared proffer such insolent remarks to his master. Khair ed-
Din waved him aside.

"The meaning of this commotion is that Sultan Moulay Hassan has fled, and that I have taken his place," he said. "Who
are you, then, who are so apparently unaware of the events
shaking this country?"

"Ahmed ben Salem, official portraitist and painter to the
palace."

And as Khair ed-Din moved forward, he stood aside to allow him to enter.

Khair ed-Din had more than once encountered the adver-
sary he had just overcome. He felt nothing but contempt for
Moulay Hassan, unworthy heir to the prestigious Hafsid dy-

nasty. A puny man who cut a wretched figure, he had seemed to bend under the weight of the crown and the royal mantle of his ancestors. He was certainly doomed to defeat and humiliation when confronted by the terrible pirate, master of the Mediterranean!

But now the defeated sultan was here, on the four walls of this vast room; not, however, with bent back, hung head, and feet still convulsed after his precipitate flight. On the contrary; he was seen ensconced on a rearing horse, or surrounded by his dignitaries flinging their cloaks onto the ground for him to walk over, or perched on a tower dominating the city, or even in his harem, surrounded by his favorites swooning with love.

Khair ed-Din walked around the room, his eyes ablaze with a fury that mounted one degree with each succeeding painting. He had crushed Moulay Hassan. Driven him out of his palace with ignominy. Obliged him to flee so that you couldn't see him for dust, leaving everything behind him, even down to the meat revolving on the spits. And now, thanks to this devil of a painter, the conquered man was still on his walls, triumphant, royal, ablaze with all his glory.

"To prison!" he finally snarled. "And throw all these daubs into the fire!"

Then he went out abruptly, while his soldiers surrounded Ahmed ben Salem and covered him with fetters.

In the weeks that followed, Khair ed-Din was busy consolidating and organizing the overwhelming victory that had made him the most powerful man in the whole of the Maghreb. His new victory, however, brought about a metamorphosis in him at which he was the first to be surprised. His subjection of Algiers and Algeria had already transformed the onetime buccaneer into the governor of a citadel. And now that he had become the equal of a king in this refined palace, he felt new obligations incumbent upon him. In the first place, he had realized that it was no longer appropriate for him to do anything himself. From then on, between things and himself there must always be a minister, an executive, an assistant, or at the very least a servant. This had begun with his saber. It was his oldest fighting companion, a heavy, crude weapon, whose enormous basket hilt covered his whole hand and whose broad, jagged blade contained tiny notches, in spite of its thickness. How many skulls had he not split with this swashbuckler! Tears of emotion came to his eyes when he merely caressed it with the palm of his hand! But from now on it was clear that nevermore would he split skulls, and that never again must his old brackmard dangle down his legs. He exchanged it for a short, delicate dagger with a chased hilt, whose blade he considered just about good enough to clean his nails with.

Then it was his clothes that were transformed: velvet was substituted for his coat of mail, and silk took the place of hemp.

But all this was still of very minor significance, because now here was this soldier who had a passion for action, who had never suffered a moment's doubt, whose courage and strength had always been equal to every situation—here was this new sovereign, suddenly imbued with the idea of his recent dignity, looking at himself in the mirror of royalty and finding it difficult to recognize himself.

This was when he remembered Ahmed ben Salem, and the portrait gallery in which the wretched Moulay Hassan had cut such a noble figure. Since he had adopted the little ceremonial dagger, the silk jabot and the velvet doublet, should Khair ed-Din not now have his official portrait painted? And yet this prospect, however natural for any other man, was enough to make him bristle with apprehension and horror . . .

There was an extremely good reason for this: Khair ed-Din never showed either his head, on which he wore a turban, or his chin, which was covered by a green silk bag, tied to his ears by two cords. Why these precautions? That was his secret, a secret known to all his entourage but to which no one would have dared make the slightest allusion.

In the days when he had attended the Koranic school, Khair

ed-Din had been cruelly mortified by his masters and fellow students because of the color of his hair. For years, the flaming, russet-red crest that stood up on his head had attracted gibes and blows, and, still worse, it had inspired a kind of sacred revulsion. For according to Saharan tradition, red-headed children are accursed. They are accursed because the only reason they are redheads is that they were conceived when their mother had "the curse." Thus they bear the obvious and indelible mark of that infamy, for it is quite simply this impure blood that has dyed their hair. And the shame extends to the whole of their skin—milky yet freckled—to every single one of their hairs, and even to their smell . . . and Khair ed-Din's classmates had moved away from him, holding their noses.

The child had suffered martyrdom. When he grew older, though, his strength had made him formidable. Finally, when he was old enough to wear a turban, he was able to conceal the cause of all the outrage. But it had all begun again only a few years later, when his beard had grown; it was not russet-colored like his hair, but definitely red, as if it were made of copper wire. He had then imposed the fashion of the beard bag, an accessory from which he was never parted, and which his courtiers had docilely adopted.

He was nevertheless always on the watch to see where other people were looking, and if their gaze happened to linger on his chin, his hand immediately clenched the hilt of his saber. The Roumis had nicknamed him Barbarossa, and he thought it just as well for their heads that they lived on the opposite shore of the Mediterranean. Khair ed-Din was so sensitive on this particular point that his intimates were always careful not to mention certain words in his presence—fox, squirrel, bay horse—and everyone knew that he was always in a vile mood on the nights when a huge, reddish moon was floating in a murky sky.

And now, at the pinnacle of his power, he was discovering the force of the image, and that a king cannot avoid looking at himself in a mirror. One morning, then, he had Ahmed ben Salem taken out of his prison and brought before him.

"You told me that you were the official portraitist and painter to the palace," he said.

"Certainly, seigneur. Such is my office; such is my title."

"Your office and your title, yes. But what is your function?"

"In the first place, I have to paint the portraits of the high dignitaries of the court. I also have to reproduce the architectural beauties and the splendors of the palace, so that throughout space and time, no one shall remain in ignorance of them."

Khair ed-Din nodded. That was just what he expected of the artist.

"But tell me: suppose the high dignitary you are portraying were to be afflicted with a physical blemish, a wart, a broken nose, a menacing look or a blind eye, or something of the sort. Would you reproduce this deformity exactly, or would you try to conceal it?"

"Seigneur, I am a portraitist, not a courtier. I paint the truth. My honor is called fidelity."

"Hence, in your concern for fidelity, you would not hesitate to let the entire world know that your king has a wart on his nose?"

"I would not hesitate, no."

Khair ed-Din, feeling vaguely challenged by the intrepid pride of the painter, became red with anger.

"And would you not fear that your head might become unsteady on your shoulders?"

"No, seigneur, for the moment he saw his portrait the king would feel that I had honored, not ridiculed him."

"How so?"

"Because my portrait would be the very portrait of royalty."

"And the wart?"

"It would be so royal a wart that there would be no one who would not be proud to bear a similar one on his nose."

Khair ed-Din was deeply disturbed by these words, which were so akin to his preoccupations. He turned his back on the painter and withdrew to his apartments. But Ahmed was permitted to return to his studio. The very next day Khair ed-Din went to see him there, and questioned him anew.

"I still do not understand," he said, "how you can faithfully reproduce a face that has been rendered ugly and ridiculous by a deformity, without at the same time revealing and proclaiming its ugliness and ridiculousness. Do you really claim that you never attenuate the deformities of your models?"

"I never attenuate," Ahmed affirmed.

"And you never embellish?"

"I do indeed embellish, but without hiding anything. On the contrary, I emphasize, I accentuate all the features of a face."

"I understand less and less."

"What has to be done is to bring time into play in the portrait."

"What time?"

"You look at a face. You see it for one minute, for two at the most. And during that very short time the face is at the mercy of arbitrary concerns, absorbed by commonplace cares. After which, your memory will retain the image of a man or a woman debased by vulgar irritations. Suppose, however, that this same person comes and poses in my studio. Not for one minute or two, but for twelve times one hour, spread over a whole month, for example. The image I create of him will be cleansed of the impurities of the moment, of the thousand little daily aggressions, of the petty, contemptible actions that the banality of domestic life inflicts on everyone."

"Your model will become bored in the desert of your studio, and his face will reflect nothing but the void in his soul."

"Certainly, if it is a man or woman of no account. And in that case, yes, I shall portray on my canvas the absent air that is indeed the mask of certain people when they are no longer harassed by the outside world. But have I ever claimed to paint the portrait of a nobody? I am the painter of the depths, and the depths of a human being are transparent on his face once the agitation of day-to-day life ceases, as the rocky depths of the sea, with their green algae and golden fish, appear to the eyes of the voyager when the surface is no longer rippled by the oarsmen or by a changeable wind."

Khair ed-Din remained silent for a moment, and Ahmed, who had not taken his eyes off him, began to suspect for the first time the secret wound concealed under the triumphs of the adventurer.

"This soul you discover and portray on your canvas—is it very different from one man to another? Or does it contain something that is common to all men?"

"It is very different, yet at the same time there is indeed a common bond, something that derives from human nature itself. Some, for instance, are possessed by a great love—whether happy or unhappy. Others are forever immersed in a dream of beauty, a beauty they seek on all sides, a reflection of which they sometimes find here or there. Still others engage in a dialogue with God, and ask no other felicity than that formidable, tender Presence. Others again . . ."

"And what about kings? What is the attribute of a royal soul?"

"The king reigns, and the king governs. And these functions are very different, diametrically opposed, even. For the king who governs has to do battle, day after day, hour after hour, against poverty, violence, lies, treachery, rapacity. Now, in theory he is the stronger, but in practice he is confronted by formidable adversaries, and if he is to conquer them he is forced to turn their own unjust arms against them—violence, lies, treachery. And he, and even his crown, is besmirched by them. Whereas the king who reigns shines like the sun, and like the sun he spreads light and warmth around him. The king who governs is seconded by a cohort of hideous torturers who are called the means. The king who reigns is surrounded by a bevy of beautiful young women, white and perfumed, who are called the ends. It is sometimes said that these young women justify these torturers, but that is one more of the torturers' lies. Must it be added that I paint the king who reigns, and not the king who governs?"

"But what, I ask you, are ends without means?"

"Not a great deal, I agree, but of what value are means when they have caused their ends to be forgotten, and when they have even destroyed them by their ferocity? Indeed, the life of a king is a perpetual fluctuation between these two terms. Moulay Hassan passed for a weak, irresolute man. That was because he could not bear the image of himself that he saw reflected in the eye of the torturer, the victim, or the ordinary soldier. So he came to see me, and when I say he came to see me, it was far more that he came to see himself here. When he came in he was pale, discouraged, nauseated by the vile deeds of his profession. He looked at his portraits, the ones you caused to be destroyed. In their light, he cleansed himself of all the defilement of power. I could see him swelling anew with his kingly pride. He regained confidence in himself. I did not need to utter a single word of comfort. He smiled at me, and when he left he was restored to equanimity."

This evocation of his enemy visibly displeased Khair ed-Din. Was it possible, without impertinence, to compare him with that nincompoop? And yet it was in his bed that he was sleeping, it was with his portraitist that he was conversing!

"And what about the common bond which, you said, exists between all men?"

"When you silence the tumult of daily life so that you hear only the voice of the soul, even though this voice is utterly individual, personal, unlike any other, there is nevertheless one characteristic which is common to all men and which proves to you that this voice—when it exists, of course—is its deepest song."

"What characteristic?"

"Nobility."

Khair ed-Din was silent again for a moment, reflecting on everything Ahmed had just said. Finally he walked over to the studio door and, on the point of disappearing, he turned and said:

"Tomorrow morning, an hour after sunrise, you will start my official portrait."

He was going through the door, but once again he had second thoughts:

"In black and white," he specified.

The next day, Ahmed was ready for him. He stood in an immaculate robe in front of a vast panel made of strips of overlapping and superimposed papyrus rubbed with cedar oil. On a low table within his reach were clusters of feathers, bundles of charcoal, and bottles of India ink. There were also pellets of soft bread for the shading, and the shellac dissolved in spirits that is pulverized on a drawing as a fixative. All that was missing was the model. He did not appear.

Ahmed waited the whole day for him. When night fell his panel was covered with sketches he had tossed off to relieve his boredom. Together they formed a rough portrait of Khair ed-Din done from memory, which meant that it represented the idea of Khair ed-Din that had taken shape in the painter's mind. Whether because of this abstract and symbolic origin, or because it was reduced to black hatching on a white ground, all that emanated from this figure was an impression of force, of brutality, even. This worried Ahmed. He wondered why his new master had not come to pose, and why the portrait—which he had been obliged to paint without a model—was to such a degree devoid of the majestic serenity that is alone appropriate to a sovereign. He realized, however, that these two questions demanded one and the same answer, when on the third day Khair ed-Din suddenly burst into his studio and, standing squarely in front of the sketch of his portrait, legs apart and hands on hips, burst into savage laughter.

"I see," he said, "that you haven't the slightest need of my presence to make my portrait! And believe me, it's just as well. In the first place because the idea of offering myself up to your indiscreet gaze for hours on end is totally repugnant to me.

And in the second place because this portrait of me, alive as it is with brutal force, greatly delights me."

"Seigneur," replied Ahmed, "I do need your presence to make a real portrait of you, a royal portrait, symbolizing your sovereignty over your subjects and your lands. And that is not all: this portrait must be in color. And I still have one more demand to make."

"What demand?" roared the former pirate.

"You must agree to remove your turban, and also . . ."

"And what else?" yelled Khair ed-Din.

"And also your beard bag," said Ahmed courageously.

Khair ed-Din hurled himself on him, brandishing his dagger. But he remembered in time that this ludicrous weapon was purely ceremonial. He sheathed it with fury, turned on his heel and disappeared, followed by his courtiers, who, by the expressive glances they darted at the painter, showed fairly clearly that they didn't give much for his chances.

Ahmed was profoundly shaken by this scene. He expected to be taken back to prison, but no soldier appeared in the days that followed. Actually, though, the silence and isolation in which he was left were more agonizing than a precise threat. He tried to return to his work. But every touch he added to Khair ed-Din's portrait intensified his air of ferocity, which was hardly surprising after his last visit.

Finally Ahmed decided to go and consult a woman in whom he had the greatest confidence—if, that was, they allowed him to leave, for she lived in a far-off oasis in the middle of the desert. Nobody seemed to take any notice of him, however, either when he ventured out of his studio or when he left the palace, and he found it disconcertingly easy to set off along the track with a servant and two camels.

Kersten, like Ahmed, was an artist, and he therefore thought of her as a kind of sister, although in every other respect she was as different from him as day is from night. Blonde and blue-eyed, she was a native of Scandinavia and had brought with her an art that had its origins in the cold. In her villa with its low white outhouses, half hidden under the palms, it was possible to glimpse the complicated shapes of huge looms, made of a wood unknown in Africa, Norway maple. On these marvelously perfected devices, she produced, hour after hour and with infinite patience, snow-covered landscapes, hunting scenes with sleighs, icebound fortresses, figures dressed in furs the like of which no African had ever seen or even imagined. Ahmed sometimes took her one of his paintings. Using it as a cartoon, with her consummate skill she turned it into a tapestry which, although certainly extremely faithful, was also enriched with such depth and tenderness that he could hardly recognize his own work thus transfigured. Because its material is wool—the softest and warmest product of animal life—tapestry celebrates the great reunion of naked man with lost animality and its silks, its down, its fleeces.

Kersten welcomed Ahmed, as usual, with the familiarity appropriate between artists, tempered by the reserve due to her Nordic origin. Ahmed had brought his charcoal portrait of Khair ed-Din with him. He told his friend all he knew about and had endured from the erstwhile pirate, now the master of Tunis. Kersten seemed keenly interested in the extreme touchiness he manifested with regard to his beard and hair. They devised a plan, decided that she would come and visit him as soon as possible, and Ahmed set out on the return journey to Tunis, having exchanged his charcoal drawing for a tapestry square representing a full-blown sunflower, which the men of the north, deprived of sunlight, cultivate for their solar splendor.

Khair ed-Din was away from Tunis for several months, subjugating the south of the country. When he returned, he was at the zenith of his glory. He had every reason to believe that he had founded a dynasty that would last for a thousand years. Hence the necessity to settle the irritating question of his official portrait had become even more acute. One morning, therefore, he burst into Ahmed's studio. He immediately looked for the charcoal portrait he had appreciated on his last visit and which, furthermore, seemed to have brought him luck.

"It was only a sketch," Ahmed explained. "I haven't got it anymore."

"You dared to destroy it?" Khair ed-Din shouted, as if it were a question of an attempt on his person.

"On the contrary," said Ahmed. "I made a present of it to a woman of genius, because I was certain that she would turn it to the best account."

"What account?"

For all response, Ahmed went over to one of the studio walls, over which there was a hanging. With a sweeping gesture he uncovered it. Khair ed-Din uttered an exclamation. Behind the hanging, a vast, long-wool tapestry had appeared. Woven entirely in varying shades of russet, it represented a European landscape in autumn, a forest interior buried under dead leaves where foxes were creeping, squirrels leaping, and a herd of deer fleeing. But that was still nothing. To the spectator standing at a distance and paying more attention to the overall picture than to the details, it seemed that all this symphony in russet major was in reality only a portrait, a face, the abundance of whose hair and beard provided the material for this whole forest world—animal fur, foliage of trees, plumage of wildfowl. It was, yes, Khair ed-Din's portrait, reduced to its primary color, every shade of which, from the palest to the most deeply dyed, caressed the eye with exquisite tenderness.

"How harmonious it is," murmured Khair ed-Din, after a long, admiring silence.

"The artist comes from the north of Europe," Ahmed thought he should explain. "She is evoking a landscape in her country in the month of October, when hunting is resumed. That is the most royal of all the Nordic seasons."

"It's my portrait," Khair ed-Din insisted.

"No doubt, seigneur. Such is Kersten's artistry that, starting from my charcoal sketch, and having a simple Scandinavian autumn landscape in mind, she immediately understood the profound affinity of your face with that landscape, and so incorporated your portrait into the forest interior in such a way that no one can be quite sure what is foliage and what is hair, what is reynard and what is beard."

Khair ed-Din had gone up to the wall and was passing both his hands over the tapestry.

"My hair," he stammered, "my beard . . ."

"It is indeed your very self, restored to your dignity of king of the trees, of king of the animals, thanks to your fleece, your fur, your mane," said Ahmed.

And he remembered Kersten's mysterious remark, when he had mentioned Khair ed-Din's red hair and its ignominious origin: "What has been done by a woman, only the hands of a woman can undo," she had said.

The better to relish his own tenderness, Khair ed-Din had pressed his cheek against the tapestry. Turning his head, he plunged his face into it.

"What a beautiful, profound odor!" he exclaimed.

"The odor of nature, the odor of russet," said Ahmed. "It's the wool of wild sheep, washed in a mountain torrent and dried on euphorbia bushes. Yes, that is the great superiority of tapestry to painting: a tapestry is designed to be seen, it's true, but also to be felt, and even to be smelled."

Then Khair ed-Din did something unprecedented, the novelty of which filled his accompanying courtiers with terror: abruptly, he snatched off the green silk bag covering his beard and hurled his vast turban to the ground. Then he shook his head like a wild animal that wants to flourish its mane.

"Barbarossa!" he roared. "My name is Sultan Barbarossa! Spread the word! I desire this tapestry to appear in the place of honor behind my throne in the great hall."

The next day,[1] Sultan Moulay Hassan, who had rallied the Italian princes, the Pope, and the Emperor Charles V to his

[1] July 14, 1535.

cause, retook Tunis with an army of thirty thousand men, borne by a fleet of four hundred sail.

Khair ed-Din took refuge in Europe, the land of russet autumns, where he became the friend of the king of France, François I. He had many more adventures, but never again did he hide his hair or his beard.

Five

HAD ZETT ZOBEIDA also remained among the crowd to listen to the storyteller, Abdullah Fehr? Idris had looked around for her, but then, carried away by the tale, he had given up. Now that everyone was standing in silence, he couldn't resist the attraction of the Chraïa fortress, where the musicians were installed. He walked silently up to the outer walls of the ksar. There were two tents, enlivened by occasional glimmers of light. He could hear murmurs, a baby whimpering, muffled laughs. Suddenly a dog began to bark furiously. Then there was a man's voice ordering it to keep quiet. Shortly afterward, a stone came whistling past Idris's ears and scattered some of the debris near him. He beat a hasty retreat. But later, back on the terrace of the family house, he remained for a long time gazing up into the black sky, unable to sleep. Cricket, dragonfly, skit, script—the old ritornello still danced in his head, and he could still see the mute discourse of Zett Zobeida's naked belly. But Kersten, the blonde woman who had come from the north with her multicolored wools, had given images a softness that had reconciled the most physically ill-favored man to his own portrait. Would Kersten have succeeded as well with a camera? Certainly not. What would Idris think of himself in the photo taken by the blonde woman? He must have slept a little, for he didn't see the sky turn pale, and the eastern horizon was becoming pink when he got up. He simply had to return to the musicians' camp. He had to see Zett Zobeida again. He ran to the Chraïa ksar. A sense of prudence made him slow down and hide when he got to the first ruins behind the derelict walls. Unnecessary precaution—the two tents had disappeared. Idris went into the campsite. There remained only the fires, all extinguished but still smoking, rotting fruit, turds, indefinable vestiges that Idris turned over with his naked foot. An indescribable melancholy descended on his heart. He must leave. He wanted to leave with her. Like the blonde woman in her Land-Rover. He must leave—or else marry according to the rites. But leave, rather: leave!

Suddenly Idris saw something glittering in the sand between his toes. He bent down and picked up Zett Zobeida's most beautiful jewel, the golden droplet on its broken thong. He rolled it around in the hollow of his hand. He held it up on the end of its thong and made it dance in the rising sun.

> The cricket's wings bear a script
> The dragonfly's wings bear a skit . . .

The haunting music came back to his ears, and Zett Zobeida's dance . . . Zett Zobeida, the black woman with the abstract, absolute jewel that had no model in nature. He himself danced in the young morning light, in the middle of that befouled ground.

Then he pushed the golden droplet into his pocket, and fled.

Six

TWO DAYS LATER, it was Salah Brahim's day. He made the return journey from Beni-Abbès to Tabelbala and back—three hundred kilometers—in his old Renault truck, bringing the oasis dwellers their mail and everything they had ordered on his previous visit: tools, medicines, clothes, and even salt and seeds, a whole cargo whose increase from year to year was a measure of the declining self-sufficiency of the oasis. His arrival in the late morning—he left Beni-Abbès at dawn—was always something of an event. The delivery, to which he proceeded with all his natural flamboyance, made him a popular character, even though a little feared or despised by some. He was the principal living link with the outside world, and his attitude toward the oasis dwellers differed according to whether or not they had ever been away from the oasis. Toward those who had never left Tabelbala, he affected a protective familiarity and a superior air which impressed many, but exasperated some. In the eyes of the young who dreamed of emigrating, he shone with an indisputable, though somewhat suspect, prestige.

Idris knew that his photo couldn't possibly be in the mail now arriving, only four days after the passage of the Land-Rover. He nevertheless went to watch the delivery, for that was how he would receive it, and henceforth every delivery concerned him, and would concern him ever more as the arrival of the photo became more likely. How long would he have to wait? Three, five, seven weeks? Unfortunately, his mute presence at each delivery couldn't escape Salah Brahim's notice, and after the third one the driver began to pick on him and make allusions to the far-off fiancée from whom Idris was desperately—he maintained—expecting a love letter. Then he suited the action to the words. "Here it is, here it is," he exclaimed, brandishing an envelope. After which he pretended to be deciphering the name of the addressee with some difficulty, and then concluded, with a mournful air: "Well, no, my poor Idris, it still isn't for you. But the name is rather like yours, you know. You're on fire, Idris, you're on fire; be patient a bit longer!" The oasis dwellers standing around him roared with laughter at these pleasantries.

In the end, Idris no longer dared show his face when the truck, white with dust, drew up in front of the small waiting crowd. But he promised a handful of dates to one of the neighbors' children for each time he went to the delivery, and a pocketknife on the day he brought him his letter. And so he leapt to his feet one morning when he saw the child rushing up to him, out of breath: "It's come! It's come! Your letter's arrived!" But Salah Brahim had refused to entrust it to him. He claimed that he could hand it over only to the person it was addressed to. "But you'll give me the knife all the same?" the child begged.

Idris walked up to the truck with all the deliberation required by what remained of his dignity after the driver's jokes. At first, Salah Brahim pretended not to see him, and went on calling out names. Finally, after the last parcel had left the truck, he held up a fat envelope covered with postmarks and ringed round with several strips of sticky paper, and yelled

Idris's name to the four winds. The laughs began to ring out. Idris went up.

"Is it really you?" Salah Brahim inquired, with comic insincerity. "Are you really Idris, the person this love letter, come from the furthermost bounds of the sea, is addressed to?"

Idris had to submit to a grotesque interrogation that made the men surrounding the truck howl with laughter. At last he was given the letter, and everyone fell silent as he began to tear the envelope open. When he had done so, he pulled out a brightly colored king-sized postcard: it represented a donkey adorned with pompons and braying at the top of its voice, its head raised, baring all its teeth. Salah Brahim pretended to be astonished, in the midst of a storm of laughter and applause.

"Is that your fiancée? Or is it *your* photo?"

Idris flung the postcard down and fled, holding back tears of rage. This was the first image the entry of the Land-Rover woman into his life had bestowed on him.

Seven

DID LANCE SERGEANT MOGADEM wonder why his nephew Idris had been hanging around his gourbi for some time and paying him shy visits? Had the story of the Land-Rover, which Kuka had spread all over the oasis, reached even him? Nothing was less sure, but anyway, why should it have interested him? He enjoyed an unquestionable prestige in Tabelbala because of his military past, his ex-serviceman's pension and the relative prosperity it ensured him. But he was a recluse. He had always refused to marry, which was enough to make him something of an outsider, and it had never occurred to anyone to put his name forward for election to the djemaa to replace a member who had died. Yet there had been a time when he had taken an interest in his nephew, and he had taught him not only to speak French but also to read and write it in rudimentary fashion.

That day he was cleaning the disassembled pieces of a rifle when Idris sidled into his house. As was their wont, they didn't exchange a single word of greeting. Idris, leaning against the wall, watched him for a moment.

"Is that the rifle you used in the war?" he finally asked.

"Oh no! Not likely!" said Mogadem. "A war rifle is something quite different. This one is only just about good enough for small birds."

He laughed and, picking up its barrel, he shut one eye and looked through it as if it were a spyglass.

"Is it good for gazelles too?" Idris wanted to know.

"For gazelles, for camels, and even for robbers. For soldiers, you need a real rifle. In Italy I had a 7.5 mm with a folding bayonet and a five-round magazine. The Germans, though— they almost all had submachine guns. Submachine guns, now —they really pepper you. They're good for door-to-door stuff in a town. But they have neither range nor precision. For long-distance shooting, there's nothing like the rifle."

While he was speaking, Idris was walking up and down the room. He knew nothing more luxurious or more comfortable than his uncle Mogadem's house. The walls were bristling with hunting trophies, gazelles' heads with their horns, a stuffed kite, an ostrich-feather fan, the head of a fennec opening its little red mouth. On a packing case covered with garnet-colored velvet there was a battery wireless set that Idris had never heard working because—as Mogadem had explained— you can pick up the transmitters properly only at night. But what especially caught Idris's attention was a glass-covered frame containing the Croix de Guerre and a fuzzy, yellowed photo in which an astonishingly young Mogadem was to be seen with two of his pals, all three smiling in their beautiful uniforms.

"You might well look at that photo! It must be the only photo that exists in Tabelbala. Although there used to be one of Mustapha, taken when he went on honeymoon to Algiers. He'd had himself photographed with his wife. But I rather think that photo has disappeared. Maybe his mother-in-law burned it. The old people here don't much like photos. They believe that a photo brings bad luck. The old people are superstitious . . ."

[44]

"And don't *you* believe a photo can bring bad luck?" Idris asked.

"Yes and no. My idea, you see, is that you must hold on to a photo, you must master it," he said, making the gesture of grasping something with both hands. "That's why Mustapha had nothing to fear from the photo taken in Algiers: it was pinned onto the wall. They could see it every day. Just like this one. I keep an eye on it, stuck there under its glass. But you know, that photo has quite a story. A tragic story. Just listen to this. We were on stand-down in a village near Cassino. One of the guys there was an army photographer. He took me with these two pals. There were several different sections on stand-down, and the two guys he took with me came from a different section from mine. But we knew each other. When we were on stand-down we met up. We had fun together. Two days later, I met the photographer. He pulled an envelope out of his pocket and gave it to me. It contained three copies of the photo. "They're for you and your pals," he told me. "You can give them both their photo." I thanked him, and waited until I met the other two. I never got the chance. A couple of days later we all went to the front line. It was April 30, 1944. I'm not likely to forget the date. We were launching a new attack on the Germans entrenched in the Monte Cassino monastery. The Americans had already come to grief there at least twice. Now it was our turn. What a massacre! On both sides—both Allies and Germans. That was where I won my Croix de Guerre. You can well imagine that I'd forgotten the photos! Even so, I still had them on me, nice and warm against my chest—and that's an important detail. The following week we were on stand-down again. I went and looked for my two pals' section. It had taken a hell of a bashing. Well, after making some inquiries, I finally heard that they'd both been killed . . ."

He studied the framed photo on the wall in silence.

"This story made me think, you know. It's my opinion that because I was carrying the photo on me, it more likely brought me luck. The others, my two pals, obviously it wasn't their fault, but they'd parted with their image. That's something you shouldn't do. I can't help thinking that if I'd been able to give them both their photo, maybe nothing would have happened to them."

"What did you do with their photos, then?" Idris asked.

"I gave them to their section leader to send to their families. They were Algerians, one from Tlemcen, the other from Mostaganem."

Idris wondered whether his uncle knew about his own story of the photo taken by the blonde woman. He had no more doubts when Mogadem, after a silence, and looking him straight in the face, said:

"No. Photos, you see—you must hang on to them. Mustn't let them go gallivanting!"

Eight

TO LEAVE. To take the road north, like so many others from Tabelbala, and also from Djanet, from Tamanrasset, from In Salah, Timimoun, El-Goléa, from all those green patches on the yellow and brown map of the desert. This was what he was being advised to do by the brutal death of Ibrahim, the silhouette of the blonde woman, the legend of Khair ed-Din, the taunts of Salah Brahim, and even the story of his uncle Mogadem. But it was also the upsurge of an old nomadic atavism that was not satisfied with a future rooted in birthplaces, in the shifting prison, all the more fearsome in that it is so snug, that a wife and children create around a man. No, he had definitely made up his mind not to marry. And anyway, he had an excellent alibi in his poverty. Where could he find the dowry that a young man has to pay his future father-in-law, unless he went and worked in the north? He likewise promised his mother, who had been a widow for three years and who was alarmed at the departure of her oldest child, that he would send her a portion of his earnings. In that way she and his five brothers and sisters would not be left unprovided for.

And he cited the example of six oasis dwellers who at irregular intervals sent money orders to their families via the grocer in Tabelbala. This was the case with a distant cousin, Achour, a merry, generous lad, who had left Tabelbala several years before to go and work in Paris but had always remained in touch. They would write and tell him that Idris was coming, and then the boy would have an address, and someone he knew, in Paris.

It was quite naturally his uncle Mogadem whom he first told of his decision to leave soon. He found him wearing an army forage cap and smoking his pipe, sitting on the ledge that forms a kind of bench at the bottom of the outside walls of the gourbis. Mogadem was in no hurry. He went on peacefully sucking at his pipe, gazing into space. Finally he decided to speak.

"Is it true what they're saying? You're leaving?"

"Yes, I'm going north to look for work."

"Are you going to Beni-Abbès?"

"Yes, and then farther."

"To Béchar?"

"Yes, and then farther."

"You want to cross the sea and go to Marseille?"

"Not only to Marseille."

"You want to go to Paris?"

"To Paris, yes, to look for work."

For a long moment Mogadem seemed interested only in the way his pipe was drawing. Then he raised his head, his eyes screwed up, and looked at his nephew ironically.

"To look for work? It wouldn't more likely be a blond woman you're going to look for in Paris?"

"I don't know."

"Do you really not know?"

"Maybe it's the same thing."

Nine

MOGADEM WAS CLOSE ENOUGH to Idris to understand what he meant. The north, work, money, and platinum blondes—they were all part of the same whole, confused but glittering. The opposite of Tabelbala, somehow. But there was still something else, and Mogadem knew that better than anyone.

"Well, I'll tell you what it is you're going to look for in the north. You're going to look for that photo they took of you, which will never come to Tabelbala on its own. Go and fetch your photo, then. Bring it back here and pin it on the wall in your room, like mine here. It's better that way. After that, you'll be able to marry and have children. Unless you'd rather be alone, like me."

Idris went and sat down beside him. They didn't exchange another word, but their thoughts were probably following the same lines. They were imagining the Tabelbala Idris becoming the Beni-Abbès Idris, the Béchar Idris, the Oran Idris, the Marseille Idris, the Paris Idris, and then finally coming back to his point of departure on this earthen bench. Outwardly, no doubt, he would look just like the old men of the oasis whose sleepy eyes no longer see their surroundings because they have never seen anything else. But he would have eyes that saw; they would have been sharpened by the sea and the big city, and enlightened by silent wisdom.

Ten

HIS MOTHER had made him put his naked foot down in the doorway of their house, where she had bathed it with a little water. "So that your foot remembers this doorway, and brings you back to it," she had said. And now he had gone. He was walking along the track going northeast, the one that led to Beni-Abbès. But he had still not finished with Tabelbala. Just as he was leaving the oasis he was joined by Orta, his neighbors' saluki. It was a noble, thoroughbred animal. It had had its paws branded to protect it from the evil eye. When Idris went to check the traps he had set for the fennecs and woodcocks, he was pleased and proud to have the golden hound gamboling around him. Orta began to fawn on him. If the boy was leaving the oasis, didn't it mean that he was going hunting? Idris stopped and ordered it to go back to the village. The hound kept on running around him, its ears flattened, its tail lashing. Idris was obliged to make the gesture it feared: he picked up a stone. The dog slunk off, whining. Idris threatened it. The dog fled, its tail between its legs. Idris continued on his way. He ought to have been spared that. This last scene hurt him more than all the rest.

He knew he wouldn't have to walk the hundred and fifty kilometers to Beni-Abbès. No one ever walks for long on a desert track. There is a law of aid and friendship on desert tracks. And Idris walked, with the rising sun on his right and a crescent moon on his left, knowing that in a minute, in an hour, or when the sun was blazing down on his head in all its silent fury, he would be picked up by some vehicle and taken to his destination. His dream was that it might be a Land-Rover driven by a blonde woman—one of the blonde women who capture images in a box—but this time it would be the entire boy she would take. There wouldn't be a man sitting beside her, so Idris would be a welcome companion for her. Is it right for a woman to cross the desert alone? In any case, she would quickly tire of driving her heavy car weighed down with all its desert equipment and she'd soon be glad to hand the wheel over to her young companion, who would thus become both the master of the vehicle and the protector of the woman.

He had reached this point in his reveries when the distant rumble of an engine made him stop. Behind him, a black dot on the track was creating a vast cloud of dust. To stop walking would be a very clear request for a lift in the vehicle. Here, they know nothing of the raised-thumb sign used by European hitchhikers. You just wait, that's all. Idris stopped and waited. Then, suddenly, he was horrified. He had recognized, puffing and blowing, Salah Brahim's old Renault truck. His first reflex was to flee the track as fast as his legs would carry him. But the driver had certainly recognized him, and such a flight would be beneath his dignity. So he started walking again, keeping his back obstinately turned to the truck, thus clearly demonstrating that he was not expecting to be picked up, that he would ask no favor of the loud-mouthed driver who had so cruelly ridiculed him. If the truck stopped even so, it would be Salah Brahim who had become the petitioner.

Idris heard the increasing din of the old wreck as it came nearer. It cost him an effort not to turn his head. All the same, he couldn't stop himself from keeping well over to his right, for it was far from reassuring to feel the monster charging up behind him with all its metal sheets, chains, axles, and pistons clanking. Was Salah Brahim going to stop? No. On his left, Idris saw the beast's steaming snout pass him, the ferruginous, clattering mass go by, and he was immediately enveloped in a cloud of dust. He just had time to make out the rear tarpaulin before it disappeared. Then suddenly, there was no more noise. The dust dispersed. The truck had stopped. The left-hand window opened and Salah Brahim's jocular head looked out, accompanied by his naked, tattooed arms and his hairy chest in its tight-fitting army-surplus khaki pullover.

"Well, well—I was wondering who he could be, this pedestrian who's so proud that he turns his back on me! But it's Idris! So you're going north then, are you?"

"You can see I am," Idris admitted without enthusiasm.

"I'm not asking you where you're going, or why. You know how discreet I am. It's none of my business. And with me, anything that's none of my business is sacred. Otherwise, how could I do this job of mine, eh, with all those letters, all those parcels? But just supposing that, seeing that you're here, you happened to be making for Beni-Abbès, eh? In that case it would be too stupid not to take advantage of Salah Brahim's truck, wouldn't it?"

So saying, he had opened the right-hand door, and jerked back into the driver's seat. Idris could only, reluctantly, climb in. After all, he hadn't asked any favors. The driver seemed to be feeling well disposed toward him. Could it be that he had had some pangs of conscience about the donkey business, or did he want to play another trick on the boy?

"I can't stop anywhere for long," he explained, getting into gear. "When it ticks over, the engine heats up. And if I turn it off, there's no telling whether it will start again. Some people, you know, talk about retiring. But me, I shall only retire when my truck lets me down. It'll be an enforced retirement, because I can't see how I'd ever be able to replace my truck. But I can't help wondering what will become of the Belbalis when Salah Brahim doesn't turn up anymore. Though it's true that there won't be anyone left in Tabelbala by that time. Today, you are leaving. Last month it was your cousin Ali that I took. And three months before that I picked up four fellows walking like you on the northbound track. Some people are already wondering when this migration will stop. What I say is: it'll stop when there are only old men and old women left in the oasis. You'll ask me: what is there for a young person to do in Tabelbala? No cinema, no television, not even any dances. Work? Dates and goats, that's all. Not surprising, then, that the young people leave. Mind you, it's never me that gets them to leave the oasis. Oh no! Not crazy, Salah Brahim isn't! I'm only too well aware of what people would think, and what would happen to me one day or another, if I got the reputation of taking the young away from the oasis! There's already some who don't like me. No, the young, they leave without me, on their feet. Later, maybe, but not always, I come along with my great big broom on wheels, and I pick them up. I'm obliging, and why not? When I'm on my way from Tabelbala to Beni-Abbès, of course. Because when I come back from Beni-Abbès to Tabelbala, well, then there's never anyone on the track to give a lift to. Tabelbala is emptying, it's not filling up!"

Idris was only listening with half an ear to Salah Brahim's chatter, which melted into the racket the engine was making. Three words, however, whose fascination was irresistible, had blasted their way into his head: cinema, television, dances. With their magic phosphorescence they colored the so new, so blissful sensation of driving fast, sitting in a comfortable seat, a couple of meters above the track. No camel could replace that. How marvelous it was, this motorized, automatized modern world! In the reddish earth there were ravines, and whorls like those the ebbing tide leaves on a beach. Yet not a drop of rain had fallen for years, perhaps even for centuries. Idris, who knew this ground as his natural element, was discovering it in a different light thanks to the truck. He saw that patches of crusted sand slowed the vehicle abruptly, that ruts threw it off balance, that loose rocks loomed up on the surface of the track with diabolical suddenness. And then inevitably, but without warning, they came onto what was known as "corrugated iron." Salah Brahim let out an oath, changed gears, and stamped on the accelerator. Bouncing up and down, the vehicle charged ahead frantically. The axles shook. Salah Brahim and Idris looked at each other, their teeth chattering.

"Either I keep going at over eighty kilometers an hour," the driver said, "or else we have to go at a snail's pace."

The overtaxed old truck now seemed to be flying over all the obstacles. But the faster they went, the more bearable the vibration became. Salah Brahim skillfully avoided the most obvious potholes and bumps.

"I wouldn't be able to do that when I'm coming from Beni-Abbès with a full load," he said. "But unladen, and keeping my eyes open . . ."

Suddenly, a gazelle sprang out in front of the truck. It was galloping along with such vast, light leaps that it seemed to be playing a game. For a moment Idris thought the driver was chasing the animal, but this was only an illusion. He wouldn't have allowed himself to indulge in such a useless and dangerous childish trick. Idris was disappointed to see the gazelle darting off to the left and disappearing from sight.

"In the old days, when the truck and I were young," Salah Brahim commented, "I'd have tried to shoot it. Yes, I always had my rifle in the cab. I held the wheel in my right hand and shot with my left. But all that's well and truly over. And besides, we're going too fast for my engine. If this corrugated iron continues, we'll have to stop in ten minutes."

They didn't have to stop. After the corrugated iron they came onto a surface that was as hard as a block of cement, on which the vehicle ran smoothly. The relief was so considerable that the two men relaxed and leaned back in their seats.

"It's 'fech-fech,' " Salah Brahim said. "A crust of sand and clay. It's a piece of cake so long as the crust is able to take the weight of the truck. But when it gives, oh my! The thing'll start bucking like a goat, my brother, like a goat."

The speed and the violent rush of air through the cab might have made them forget the heat. But the landscape had the numbed look resulting from the sun beating down from on high. Salah and Idris remained silent for a long moment, a little drowsy, half conscious of having escaped the furnace by a miracle. A mirage of an oasis appeared and accentuated the sadness that an excess of light and an absence of shade bestow on a landscape. They could make out bits of walls, a broken-down sheepfold, and, behind a wizened row of palm trees, the white dome of a little marabout shrine.

"You see," Salah Brahim grunted, "it's only the dead who are at home here now. I often wonder whether Tabelbala won't be like this in a few years' time."

He had to slow down, as they had come to a zone of white sand which was as dazzling as snow.

"I've been told that to the east, near El Oued," said Salah Brahim, "all the sand is white like this. Where we come from, on the whole it's yellow. I prefer that. This white sand is bad for the truck, and it hurts your eyes too."

The vehicle was skidding and sliding from right to left as if traveling over ice. Salah Brahim muttered an oath. A man was standing motionless at the side of the track. He made no sign, but his attitude made it clear enough that he was waiting for the truck. Idris had the impression that Salah Brahim was accelerating, and indeed they passed the man at speed. But only to slow down immediately, and then stop. Leaning out of the window, Idris saw the man start running toward the truck. He was about ten meters from it when Salah Brahim got into gear and stepped on the gas again. The vehicle began to move and gather speed, outdistancing the man, who slowed down and finally stopped. Immediately the truck also slowed down and came to a halt. Once again the man began to run after them.

And once again Salah Brahim let in the clutch and drove off at speed. Disconcerted, the man stopped running and began to walk, although more quickly, along the side of the track. Yet again the truck slowed and stopped.

"Why are you doing that?" Idris asked.

"I'm under an obligation to pick him up, that's the rule. But I don't like him. So I'm making him suffer."

"What's his name?"

"I don't know."

"You don't know him, then?"

"Him, no. But he's a Tibu."

Idris asked no more. Even though he had never seen a Tibu in Tabelbala, he knew the execrable reputation of these black nomads from the Tibesti highlands whom a sedentary life had decimated, dispersed, and turned into desert vagabonds and adventurers. They were said to be lazy but indefatigable; drunkards and gluttons, but of superhuman sobriety when they were on the move; taciturn, but mythomaniac the moment they did utter a word; fiercely solitary, but robbers, rapists, and murderers the moment they were in a group. All this could be seen in the hard face with its burning gaze that was framed in the truck window. Salah Brahim roughly pulled Idris closer to him to make room for the newcomer. Then the truck moved off again, but from then on the driver maintained a hostile silence. They came to a zone of shingle, where they had to slow down to spare the tires. Then all trace of the track disappeared and the truck turned due east, for the tarred road from Adrar to Beni-Abbès could not be far off now. And indeed, it appeared an hour later, and the truck turned left onto it, going north, and it could then adopt a steady cruising speed that Idris found intoxicating.

They must have covered about a hundred kilometers when the Tibu suddenly broke the silence. He uttered a few words in a raucous dialect, whose meaning Idris guessed.

"What did he say?" Salah Brahim asked.

"He said: the road is blocked," Idris transmitted.

"That's obvious," Salah Brahim grunted. "He's noticed, as I have, that all the time we've been driving on the road we haven't passed a single vehicle. That's absolutely abnormal."

"What's blocking the road?" Idris asked.

"Oh, there's only one possibility: the Sahoura wadi. On average there's water in it once a year. We've still got a quarter of an hour on the good road. And after that: inshallah!"

And indeed, twenty kilometers farther on, the road descended into a sort of valley and plunged into a torrent of tumultuous, chocolate-colored water. The truck had to come to a halt behind a column of stationary vehicles. On the other side of the wadi, about a hundred meters away, they could see a similar column, also stationary. In the absence of a bridge, the road crossed the wadi on a cement platform about thirty centimeters high. Most of the time the crossing was dry. But that day a storm had suddenly arisen a few kilometers upstream, the water was swirling over the causeway, and it was impossible to gauge its depth with any precision. And this might last for two hours, or it might last for two days. The three men jumped out of the truck and went down to join a group conferring on the bank of the torrent. The big question was to find out whether a vehicle had any chance of crossing to the other side, taking into account both the depth and the violence of the deluge. One danger was the mud deposited on the platform and making it slippery, and another was the submersion of the exhaust pipe, which would inevitably make the engine stall. A young boy hitched up his djellaba and walked into the current, supporting himself with a pole. He took a few steps and then hurriedly returned to the bank. His legs were covered with gashes. For there was another factor: the stones washed down in the fast-moving stream.

A little farther away there was activity around an old Dodge laden with bales of wool. The driver had just fitted a rubber tube to the end of his exhaust pipe and was tying it to a rail, high enough to be out of reach of the water. He jumped up on his seat and blew his horn loudly to attract everyone's attention. Then he began to drive down the slope, and the front wheels of the Dodge plunged into the muddy stream. At first this venture seemed likely to succeed, for it looked as if the water didn't come up any higher than the wheels and was not endangering the engine's vital organs. Splashed with brown patches, the heavy vehicle moved slowly forward, swaying from side to side. It was about a third of the way over when it became obvious that it was deviating from the straight line. On that slippery surface, was it succumbing to the pressure of the current pushing it to the left, or was the driver's vision blurred by the torrent rushing in front of his windshield at breakneck speed? It must now be driving on the extreme left of the invisible platform. Then all of a sudden it tilted over to the left, first its front, then its back. The wheels had left the causeway. And the Dodge slowly toppled over and came to rest in the brown water. It couldn't have been more than a meter deep. The driver climbed out through the right-hand window and began to walk over to his cargo of wool, making great gestures of despair.

Salah Brahim and Idris went back to the Renault. The Tibu had disappeared.

"I don't know what he's up to," Salah Brahim grunted, "but if I know anything about him and his lot, I'd be highly surprised if he waited for long on this side of the wadi. Nothing has ever held a Tibu up for long."

He sat down, placed his hands on his knees, and stared lugubriously at the back of the car in front of them.

"And you want me to tell you something? Well, if you were to ask him where he's going and what he intends to do there, he wouldn't answer. Or he'd invent some cock-and-bull story. Because in actual fact, (a) he doesn't know where he's going, and (b) he has no intention of doing anything whatsoever there. That's the Tibu for you: they move around on principle, for no purpose and no reason. Total vagrancy, in short!"

He fell silent, and watched a big all-terrain Toyota moving down toward the wadi. It stopped, and the Tibu got out of it.

Salah Brahim was amazed to hear himself being told that the Toyota was going to cross, thanks to its four-wheel drive and its exhaust being on the roof, and that he, the Tibu, had persuaded the driver to take the Renault truck in tow. And suiting the action to the words, he brandished a wire towline equipped with a buffer spring.

Salah Brahim stood up, incredulous yet docile. The exchanges with the driver of the Toyota—who was English—were limited to the minimum, but confirmed what the Tibu had said. How had this devil of a man been able to concoct this solution, and above all, why was he acting in this way? All they had to do was fix the line to the front of the Renault and the back of the Toyota and then let the two vehicles slide down to the wadi. The Tibu stayed on board the Toyota. Heavy and powerful as a tank, it crossed the wadi sending up sprays of muddy water. Salah Brahim, forced to follow, grumbled that the accursed Englishman didn't need to go so fast, especially as the backwash created by the Toyota sent furious waves lashing against the front of the Renault right up to its windshield. When they got a footing on the right bank of the wadi, the two vehicles looked like two slabs of shiny mud. People milled around them. They had to get out and answer questions, receive slaps on the back and congratulations. They were helped to wash their windshields. In all this animation, Idris was probably the only one to notice a solitary man walking away from the road with a steady, light step: the Tibu.

Salah Brahim and the Englishman shook hands, and the two vehicles set off toward Beni-Abbès, soon separated by the superior speed of the Toyota. It was only an hour later that Salah Brahim began to worry about the Tibu.

"Do you think he stayed with the Englishman?" he asked.

"No," Idris replied, "I saw him walking off into the desert."

Salah Brahim thought for a moment, then suddenly braked and stopped his vehicle. He opened the glove compartment in the dashboard and took out a huge old wallet.

"The bloody swine! He's gone off with my cash!"

"How much?"

"I don't know exactly. At least twelve hundred dinars. He didn't have a wasted day!"

"But he also helped us save time," Idris argued.

"It was an expensive way to cross the wadi!"

Salah Brahim didn't say another word until they got to the first houses in Beni-Abbès. He had no time to do the honors of the town for his young companion. Two motorcycle gendarmes posted at the side of the road signaled to him to stop.

"Follow us to the gendarmerie, if you please."

And the next five hundred meters were covered under the escort of the motorbike cops. At the gendarmerie they found the Englishman from the Toyota. He had lodged a complaint. Salah Brahim's traveling companion had stolen a wad of five thousand dinars from him. Fortunately, Salah Brahim was known in Beni-Abbès. He described the encounter with the Tibu, and the theft of which he himself was the victim. The Englishman agreed that Idris was not the man he had driven in his Toyota. The inspector made merciless fun of Salah Brahim. For an English tourist to get himself robbed by a Tibu—that was understandable. But him, an old desert fox! Obviously there had been the flood at the Sahoura wadi, but that too was the desert!

When they left the gendarmerie, having given signed statements, Salah Brahim's resentment was unleashed on Idris. True, the boy was not responsible for anything that had happened during that execrable day, but Salah Brahim had picked him up at the roadside, as he had later picked up the Tibu, and that created a certain affinity between him and the Tibu. And anyway, the least that could be said was that he had not brought him luck. A traveling companion like that was best avoided. He'd know that in the future!

Idris spent the night in the yard of a kind of derelict farm belonging to the old fortress in the middle of a palm grove. Emptied of its inhabitants by the Foreign Legion at the beginning of the war,[1] this traditional village built of dried mud served as a refuge for people passing through before they managed to disappear completely. His head buzzing with the adventures of the first day of his journey, he couldn't get to sleep, what with the snores of a fat man and the whimpers of a baby clinging to its mother. He kept seeing the hard, wily face of the Tibu, surrounded by the sordid aureole he had earned by the skill with which, one after the other, he had robbed the Englishman and Salah Brahim. In Idris's imagination he was linked with his memory of Ibrahim, but he was even more prestigious. The solitude surrounding the Tibu like a dim halo was even fiercer than that of the Chaamba. Most of the time Ibrahim had lived alone with his herd of camels. But he had talked to his animals, seen to their needs, in the same way as they themselves had nourished him. He had had human exchanges with the other herdsmen and with the oasis dwellers. But the Tibu seemed to be in open or covert conflict with all his fellow men. Idris had quickly repressed the glow of sympathy he had felt when he saw the Tibu walking away with his winged gait after they had crossed the Sahoura. No, that man would not have accepted a companion, or if so, only as a ruse, with the intention of stealing from him and later abandoning him, dead or alive. He was a wild animal. No, he was not a wild animal. No animal surrounds itself with such solitude, no animal behaves with such hostile indifference toward its fellows. Only a man is capable of that. Only a man . . . Only a man. Idris finally fell asleep, and in his dream he saw Ibrahim's face merge with that of the Tibu.

PEOPLE HAD SPOKEN TO HIM of a "sea of sand." Idris had never seen the sea, but he had a very accurate image of it when, at the end of a street, he stumbled across a great dune that climbed, virgin and golden, right up to the sky. A hill at

[1] In 1957.

least a hundred meters high, soft and perfectly intact, constantly caressed and remodeled by the wind, thus heralded, as if it were its first wave, the immense ocean of the Great Occidental Erg. He couldn't stop himself from charging up this soft, shifting mountain which crumbled under his feet in golden cascades and on whose flank he lay down for a moment to catch his breath. And yet there was nothing very tiring about the climb, and he soon found himself straddling its crest, a clearly delineated ridge that was all the time being combed and sharpened by the lapping of the wind. Toward the east, the golden backbones of countless other dunes rippled as far as the horizon; a sea of sand, yes, but solidified, motionless, without a single vessel. Looking back, he saw the cubic huts at his feet, with the domes and terraces of the village and, farther away, below him, the green fleece of the palm grove. A murmur of cries, calls, barks, and then suddenly, floating above the community, the chant of the muezzin rose as if it were the sole proof of life in the oasis. On his way down he noticed that his footprints on the flank of the first dune had already been effaced, as if absorbed, digested by the depth of the sand. The dune was once again virgo intacta as on the first day of Creation. He wondered by what miracle this mass of shifting sand, constantly reshaped by the air, didn't invade the streets, didn't cover the houses. No, though, it very discreetly stopped at the foot of the little wall, only a few centimeters high, that demarcated the village.

He walked until he came to the grounds of the Rym Hotel, a sumptuous residence designed by the architect Fernand Pouillon, with a swimming pool, tennis courts, and a terrace overlooking the palm grove. At this still matutinal hour a carousel of cars and motorcycles of all makes and nationalities was revolving in front of the entrances. Idris stopped, amazed at such luxury and interested by the variety of the vehicles. He could just catch a glimpse of the terrace with its red umbrellas under which couples were gaily having their breakfast. There were bearded men in blue dungarees, soldiers in khaki uniforms, a few children shouting as they chased one another around the tables, but above all there were women, one of whom, a blonde with a high-pitched voice, resembled—but didn't equal—the one in the Land-Rover.

"Hey, you down there! You've got no business here. Go somewhere else!"

A black employee, who had been carrying the suitcases and bags of a family about to leave, was yelling at Idris, and roused him from his contemplation. It was the first time anyone had ever spoken to him in such a way. He was staggered; not because he didn't understand, but on the contrary because he was suddenly discovering, with luminous clarity, his place in this society that was so new to him. Not only did he not belong to the category of the guests of the hotel, but its servants had a right to shout at him and drive him away. He walked off, chewing over this essential verity. It was obvious, but he hadn't even suspected it a few minutes before.

He crossed the village, his eyes taking in the cafés, grocers' shops, hairdressers, craftsmen's workshops, piles of green vegetables; he was sniffed at by dogs, he was made to jump out of the way by passing cars, at the same time both amazed and wounded by the harsh words of the black employee of the Rym Hotel that were still ringing in his ears: you've got no business here, go somewhere else. He discovered the municipal swimming bath, fed by a gushing mineral spring and shaded by a screen of wisteria and bougainvillea. Some young boys were diving, and chasing one another amidst laughter and exclamations. After the Rym Hotel, here was another image of paradise, an image of coolness, of blissful nudity, of gratuitous games. He sat down at the foot of a palm tree to contemplate this picture at his leisure. One of the adolescents, glistening like a fish, passed close by him. His smiling gaze came to rest on him for an instant, and a few drops of water splashed him. Idris didn't budge. It was indeed a picture he was looking at, an exclusive scene to which he had no access. Dusty and famished, already exhausted although it was still only late morning, even though he was their age he was not the brother of these children disporting themselves with cries of joy between the green waters of the pool and the mauve clusters cascading over their heads. A young migrant from the south, embarking on an uncertain adventure that nothing must be allowed to delay, Idris had alighted there like a bird of passage.

He resumed his stroll, went down an alleyway, lingered in front of a display of confectionery. The owner of the shop was dozing in a chair, and offered him a honey cake once he had made sure that he wasn't stealing anything. He was nearing the palm grove when he found himself at the door of the Saharan Museum, an offshoot of the Arid Zones Laboratory funded by the French National Center for Scientific Research. The entrance fee was two dinars, far too much to spend out of the small amount of money he had brought with him. He was just about to go down to the palm grove again when a big air-conditioned bus drew up outside the museum. Its front and rear doors folded back and some tourists began to get out and stand around outside it. It was a conducted tour for pensioners of both sexes, and all that white hair, all those bent backs and knotted fingers clutching walking sticks, made a strange sight. The guide appeared very spry in comparison, but the juvenility he put into his role of the life and soul of the party seemed a bit forced. To the great delight of the other members of the party, he gave his arm with an air of comic gallantry to a staid, sour-looking old maid. This seemed to be a joke that had been going on since the beginning of the tour. Idris mingled with the group and found himself in the first room of the museum, which was full of glass cases and stuffed animals. Gesticulating profusely, the guide ran up and down, coming out with patter and jokes like a fairground barker. A little crowd of the faithful surrounded him and punctuated his remarks with delighted little laughs. The rest of the visitors had scattered into the other rooms and the garden. Idris listened attentively to a speech whose every phrase, every word, concerned him.

[65]

"You are here, mesdames et messieurs, and even you, made-moiselle, in order to discover the secrets of the desert and the charms of the Sahara. As you see, the desert is not so deserted as people make out, since it is inhabited by all the stuffed animals surrounding you here. Stuffed, yes, because insofar as living animals are concerned, it must be said that they have all disappeared, the victims not of the rigors of the climate but of the malevolence of man. This is notably the case with the graceful gazelle and also with the ostrich, even though the capacity of its stomach was celebrated. It is also the case with the wild sheep, the leopard, the fennec, and the porcupine. It is only as a reminder that I mention the lion, that king of the desert, the last one having been killed, as we all know, by Tartarin de Tarascon. On the other hand, here in its cage is the modest jerboa. The jerboa is—as you can see for yourselves—the extremely miniaturized result of a cross between the Aus-tralian kangaroo and the Auvergne field mouse. And to those of you who have a taste for slimy creepy-crawlies, we can offer the lizard—the monitor lizard—and the skink, the latter being known as the fish of the sands. But there is nothing to equal the grasshopper, which is as delicious when fried in oil as it is when crystallized in honey."

An old gentleman raised a timid, schoolboy finger. With a twinkle in his eye, he wanted to know whether the fish of the sands was caught with a worm or a fly.

"Excellent question!" exclaimed the guide. "I must tell you, then, that the children in the oases catch them with their bare hands, exactly like trout in a mountain stream. They eat them roasted on a bed of embers. But they also make pets of them and play with them, harnessing them to little carriages, for instance."

He moved along among the glass cases, followed by the little group of the faithful which Idris had joined. In one cor-ner there was a reconstruction of what a show card called "The Alimentary Area of the Saharan Habitat."

"And here we have the oasis dweller's kitchenette–dining

room," the guide went on. "Kitchen utensils: mortar and pestle made of acacia wood, by means of which dates, carrots, henna and myrrh are pounded into dust. When the woman has finished this task she must leave the pestle in the mortar with a few grains, so that it can feed on them after all the work it has done. Here are the sieve, the limestone grinder, and the seed sifters. And also the all-purpose dish. This is used for kneading the bread and the griddle cakes. The pitchers are for milk, the leather bottles for water, the hollowed-out gourds for cheese, clarified butter, and fat."

Idris opened his eyes wide. All these objects, of unreal cleanliness, frozen in their eternal essences, intangible, mummified, had surrounded his childhood and adolescence. Less than forty-eight hours before, he had eaten from that dish, watched his mother using that grinder.

"I see neither spoons nor forks," an old lady said in astonishment.

"That, madame, is because the oasis dweller, like our ancestor Adam, eats with his fingers. There is no shame attached to that. Everyone picks up a little handful of food with his right hand, transfers it into the hollow of his left palm, rounds it into a little pellet, and then with the thumb of his right hand pushes it to the tips of his fingers and puts it into his mouth."

And he mimed this operation, imitated by a few of the tourists, whose clumsiness raised some laughter.

"But you must not believe that the oasis dweller is therefore lacking in civility. The elementary rules of politeness in the Sahara are well known. Before every meal one must wash one's hands, and not in stagnant water, but in a spring or under a trickle of water from a pitcher held by another person. Allah's blessing must also be invoked. One does not drink while eating, but after the main dish. The water or whey then circulates clockwise, and the correct thing is to hold out both hands to grasp the pitcher or milk jug. One must not drink standing up. If one happens to be standing, one puts a knee on the ground before drinking. One must not share an egg."

Idris listened in amazement. He knew all these rules of daily life because he had always observed them, but as if spontaneously, and without ever having heard them formulated. Hearing them from the mouth of a Frenchman, while in the midst of a group of white-haired tourists, bewildered him. He had the impression that he was being forcibly removed from himself, as if his soul had suddenly left his body and was observing him from outside with astonishment.

The guide provoked general mirth when he concluded:

"And the healthy hierarchy must always be respected: the best bits go to the men, the less good ones to the women and children."

Finally they stopped in front of a glass-fronted cabinet in which jewelry and amulets were displayed.

"Here, mesdames et messieurs, you will look in vain for the head of a dog, the silhouette of a camel, a scarab, and especially for a man or a woman. No; Saharan jewels are nonrepresentational. They are abstract, geometrical forms whose value lies in signs, not images. Here are solid-silver crosses, crescents, stars, rosettes. Here are clasps, buckles, and rings made of goat's horn. The anklets are supposed to prevent the demons of the earth from climbing up a person's legs and invading the whole body. The least precious jewels are simply made of shells. The most precious are made of gold, but you will not see any of these in this museum. They were probably stolen a long time ago."

When the visitors began to leave, Idris went up to the cabinet. He had seen these silver jewels on his mother, on his aunts, on other women in Tabelbala. There were photos showing faces covered with ritual paintings to which Idris could almost have attached familiar first names. Finally, as he was moving away from the glass, he saw the reflection of a head with unruly black hair and a thin, vulnerable, anxious face: it was himself, his evanescent presence in this taxidermist's version of the Sahara.

Eleven

FROM BENI-ABBÈS TO BÉCHAR is two hundred and forty kilometers along a good tarred road, although there is nowhere to get supplies of either water or fuel. Idris had found a spare place in a taxi hired by five Mozabite merchants. They only allowed the boy to join them as an economy and because they were traveling without women. They were all grocers, recognizable by their broad, yellow, flabby faces, wearing the dark glasses that made them look fragile and shifty. Probably extremely rich, and owning opulent residences in the gardens of Ghardaïa, they pretended to be unaware of his presence during the five hours the journey lasted. They occasionally exchanged solemn remarks, with long, meditative silences in between, about the rise in price of the dried currant, the collapse of the date, the surge of the medlar, and from time to time sadly lowered their eyes to their hands encircled with ebony chaplets. Listening to them, Idris envisaged a whole horizon of shops, supermarkets, warehouses, and cargo planes, a perpetual two-way traffic of immense riches which, however, by passing through these men, had become impalpable, colorless, odorless and insipid, because they had been reduced to figures, to signs, to abstract shapes. The austerity, the discreet melancholy of these five travelers, represented opulence subjected to sobriety, commercial profits blessed by disinterestedness, success on earth sought simply as proof of obedience to the commandments of heaven. Idris was to remember this brief, bitter lesson on the mastery of things by the puritans of the desert.

And yet these solemn, suspicious men had not ignored him as completely as it seemed, and before they parted they did make a gesture toward him. They were standing by the side of the road and had just paid the taxi driver when the oldest one turned to Idris.

"I believe I understood that you were making for Marseille?" he said. "If you haven't anywhere to stay, go and see Youssef Baghabagha, who runs the Hôtel Radio, 10 Rue Parmentier, and tell him I sent you. But be sure to show him my recommendation. He only takes Mozabites and their friends."

He scribbled his name and address, with a few words of recommendation, in a notebook, tore out the page, and gave it to Idris.

FOR THE EUROPEAN, nothing could be less picturesque than Béchar—tower blocks, barracks, schools, a power station, and local government offices, the latter all the more numerous in that this chief town of the region, although it has fewer than fifty thousand inhabitants, is considered the last town worthy of the name before the start of the desert. But for Idris, it was like the discovery of a new planet. The shopwindows, the butchers' shops, and even an embryo supermarket amazed him. But most of all he was intoxicated by the motor traffic, and for quite a time he stood watching the gesticulations of a policeman on point duty. Then he discovered the station, and he couldn't tear himself away from it. Every arrival or departure of a train struck him as being a memorable event. He was sorry that he had been strongly advised to go to Oran by bus, and he spent the night on a bench in the waiting room, lulled by the intermittent din of the trains. He only fell asleep with the first glows of dawn. When, at around eight, he turned up at the bus stop, it was only to be told that the Oran bus had left at six, and that there would not be another until two days later, which would also leave at six. He had two days in front of him.

He went into a covered market, hung around in a labyrinth of alleys, emerged into a vast, dusty, deserted avenue. His lack of occupation and the hunger gnawing at his stomach made him feel as if he were floating in a slightly queasy kind of bliss. He was passing the garish façade of a shop on which uneven lettering proclaimed: "Mustapha, Photographic Artist," when he heard music and snatches of a voice coming from it. The raucous music was of the phony oriental type. With grandiloquent authority, the voice was declaiming:

"You are the sheikh, the sultan, the maharajah. You are proud. You are the great male imperial ruler. You dominate. You reign over a flock of naked women lying at your feet. Click click, all over!"

Idris had taken a few steps inside this "studio." An oriental palace was very primitively depicted on a backcloth. Around a pool with an ornamental fountain, a crowd of women in a state of chaste undress were scattered over the floor on multicolored cushions. Disguised as an oriental sultan, a young man was striking boastful attitudes. Mustapha, very fat, and wearing a red skullcap, stopped the old gramophone that had been providing the background music. The young man began to take off his oriental finery.

"The photo will be ready tomorrow evening," Mustapha promised. "That'll be fifteen dinars."

Then he noticed Idris and, being very shortsighted, took him for a new client.

"Has Monsieur come for a portrait? This is the palace of dreams. Mustapha, the photographic artist, offers to make your most extravagant fantasies come true."

But he abandoned his obsequiousness when he realized that Idris was not a client.

"What are you doing there, spying on us?"

"I was only looking."

"There's nothing for you to look at here. Go somewhere else."

Go somewhere else . . . That was the second time Idris had heard this injunction. But wasn't that precisely what he never stopped doing: going somewhere else?

"I'm trying to get some work for two days," he said, on the off chance.

"What can you do?"

"I've already been photographed. By a blonde woman."

"Well, well! A blonde woman? I suppose she was in love with you?"

"I don't know."

The young man reappeared, wearing truck driver's dungarees.

"See you tomorrow evening, then. I'll call in for my photo."

Mustapha couldn't conceal his annoyance.

"Don't forget the fifteen dinars," he muttered.

He was just about to vent his bad temper on Idris when the arrival of a couple of tourists claimed his attention. All smiles again, he hurried over to greet them.

"Messieurs-dames, Mustapha, the photographic artist, is here to make your dreams come true."

He ushered the slightly bewildered pair into his studio and began to deploy his backcloths.

"Would you like to explore the virgin forest and brave the great wild beasts of Africa? Would you like to ascend the rocky masses of the Hoggar Mountains, there to hunt wild sheep and eagles? Would you like, on the other hand, to embark on a proud sailing ship and traverse the Mediterranean?"

And each time, he displayed a gaudy, primitive backcloth.

The man tried to bring him down to earth.

"That's enough, that's enough! My wife and I are with a

group doing a conducted tour of the Sahara: Timimoun, El-Goléa, Ghardaïa."

"Well, in that case," said Mustapha enthusiastically, "I'll take you against a background of golden dunes and verdant palms. You—come over here!"

Helped by Idris, he hitched the promised Saharan decor onto a beam in the ceiling. Then he got busy with his camera. The man, shoved in front of the cloth with his wife, did try to protest, though.

"All the same, it's a bit much, going all the way to the Sahara only to get yourself photographed in a studio against a painted decor representing the Sahara!"

Mustapha interrupted his preparations and advanced on the man, one finger raised in learned fashion.

"But this, monsieur, is accession to the artistic dimension! Yes, that's what it is," he repeated with satisfaction, "accession to the artistic dimension. Every thing is transcended by its representation in an image. Transcended, yes, that's what it is. The Sahara represented on this cloth is the Sahara idealized, and at the same time possessed, by the artist."

The lady had been listening to him, entranced.

"The gentleman is right, Émile. When he photographs us in this decor, he idealizes us. It's as if we were soaring over the dunes."

"That's exactly it, that's the very word: soaring. I am going to make you soar over the dunes."

But the man remained unconvinced.

"Right. But since the real Sahara is there, I still don't see why we have to get ourselves photographed in a studio in front of a phony, painted Sahara."

Mustapha knew how to be conciliating.

"Dear monsieur, it is always possible to photograph you walking in the sand and stones with your wife. That is called amateur photography, tourist photography. What *I* do, however, is professional work. I am a creator. I re-create the Sahara in my studio, and at the same time I re-create *you*."

Then he turned to his gramophone and wound it up energetically. The sugary, languorous music made the man jump.

"Ketèlbey's *In a Persian Market!* That's all we needed!"

In the meantime, Mustapha had disappeared under his black cloth.

"Be so good, madame and monsieur, as to take up your positions in the center of the Saharan landscape. That's it, that's fine, you're in perfect focus."

He emerged into the light, with a solemn, inspired air.

"And now, madame and monsieur, the great moment has arrived. You are overwhelmed by the stern beauty of the desert landscape. You wholeheartedly accept the lesson of austerity and grandeur that arises from these sands, from these stones. You feel liberated from all your petty desires, your trivial preoccupations, your sordid cares. You are purified!"

In spite of themselves, the man and woman had adopted a solemn demeanor.

"This reminds me of our wedding day and the speech—was it the mayor or the curé who made it, I don't remember," the woman murmured.

And when Mustapha, bowing very low, promised them that their photo would be ready on the following morning, that it would be excellent, and that it would cost them thirty dinars, they shook themselves as if they had just come out of a spiritualist séance.

"All the same, there's something that intrigues me," said the man, just before they left.

"I am entirely at your service!"

"If I am not mistaken, the photo you've just taken of us will be in black and white?"

"Certainly, certainly. We professionals leave what passes for color to the amateurs."

"That's fine. But in that case, why the devil are your decors painted in color?"

The question seemed to take Mustapha unawares.

"In color?" he repeated, looking at his Saharan decor as if

he were seeing it for the first time. "You want to know why I use colored decors to produce photos in black and white?"

"Precisely."

"Well, but . . . for inspiration, obviously."

"What inspiration?"

"Mine, of course, but also that of my clients, and also, why not, that of the camera."

"The inspiration of your camera?"

"But of course; my camera participates in the creation, it too must have talent, believe me! And so I show it a landscape in color. It sees it, it likes it, and when it reproduces it, well, something of the color shows through in the black and white. Do you see what I mean?"

"No," said the man, with an obstinate air.

"But of course, Émile," his wife broke in. "The gentleman is right: he produces color with black and white. Oh, monsieur, you mustn't mind my husband, there's so little of the poet in him, you know!"

LEFT ALONE, Mustapha began to tidy up his studio, helped by Idris, who was trying to make himself useful. For a moment Mustapha worked in silence, and then returned to the subject he and Idris had previously been discussing.

"Well, then, so a blond woman photographed you?"

"Yes," said Idris eagerly. "She was in a Land-Rover that a man was driving."

"And did you like the photo?"

"I don't know. I haven't seen it yet."

"And you're going to Paris to look for a woman and a photo?"

"Do you think I shall find her?"

"Oh, if it comes to that, you'll find plenty of women and photos in Paris! Ah, if I was your age! Paris, the City of Light! The City of Images! Women and images by the million! Of course you'll find yours, that goes without saying. What's less obvious, though, is whether it'll make you any happier!"

As he spoke, he was indulging in a curious pursuit. Knitting his brow, he was rummaging in his store of backcloths. When he had finally found what he was looking for, he moved a tall mirror and put it where the camera should have been.

"It isn't for a photo," he explained. "It's just so that you can see what it looks like."

And with a mysterious air, he unrolled the backcloth he had chosen. It was Paris by night, a somewhat freakish panorama since it managed to bring together the Eiffel Tower, the Arc de Triomphe, and the Moulin Rouge, with the Seine and Notre Dame for good measure.

"Here—stand over there."

He switched on a spot.

"Look! You're in Paris, the City of Light. Lucky you! How do you like yourself?"

Idris didn't know what to say. What he saw in the mirror was a small gray silhouette, dressed in a shirt and jeans, wearing army-surplus shoes, and with an embroidered djellaba over his shoulders. Behind it was a scintillating dark-blue landscape bristling with violently lit monuments.

"If you had fifteen dinars," said Mustapha ironically, "I'd take your photo. And then you could go home. Your journey would be over. It would be less tiring, when all's said and done, than crossing the Mediterranean. But there's no point in giving you such reasonable advice. You wouldn't listen. The young always go their own way. And after all, they may be right."

So saying, he put the mirror and the Parisian backcloth away.

"If you like," he added, "you can sleep on the couch for a couple of nights. You can help me a bit tomorrow, and the next day you can get the Oran bus with the ten dinars I shall give you."

Twelve

WHEN HE GOT TO THE BUS STOP an hour early, Idris was alarmed at the number of passengers who had preceded him. Entire families burdened with very young children had clearly spent the night there with their parcels and bundles, hampers of fresh dates, and live hens confined in small wicker crates. He squatted on his heels beside an old woman who was apparently as unattached as himself and whose chin, which came right up to her nose owing to her lack of teeth, gave her a stubborn, hostile air. And there, poor among the poor, he did what the poor have an inexhaustible vocation for: he waited, motionless and patient.

The wave of satisfaction that swept through this crowd at the arrival of the bus was of short duration. Indeed, contrary to all expectations, it was already full. Where had they come from, then, all these thieves of places who were sprawling all over the seats and cluttering up the roof rack with their luggage? A long, slow process ensued whereby the bus absorbed all this humble, obstinate humanity which, the more impoverished it was, the more it was encumbered with voluminous objects. A quarter of an hour later, everyone had found some sort of place inside the bus, and the pyramid of suitcases and parcels on the roof climbed up to the stars. The bus drove off with all its lights blazing, and with great blasts on its horn made for the Place Si Kouider, crossed it, and turned into the road to Oujda. The men, women, and children packed inside it at first spent some time trying to make the best use of the exiguous amount of space allotted to each. There were a few protests, some laughs, some compromises, but after everyone had organized his own hole they all sank into patient silence. Many fell asleep. Idris found himself by a window, sitting next to the toothless old woman. She was thin, light, she had no children, a good neighbor, in short. But she didn't seem at all inclined to communicate. From time to time Idris turned away from the dark window and glanced at her. She was as immobile as a statue, her face hard and inscrutable. Her eyes, like those of a snake, never blinked.

The first gleams of the dawn, and then a pale ray of sun, provoked a certain stir in the bus. Baskets were opened. Babies woke up and began to whimper. Feeding bottles appeared. A strong smell of peeled oranges filled the air. Idris looked out of the window, which was partially misted over, and watched a still-deserted village go by. Every time the bus overtook a cyclist or a donkey, there were blasts on the horn, which they didn't even hear anymore. When he turned his head in the old woman's direction, he was surprised to see her holding out an orange to him with her left hand. She was staring at him with her lashless eyes, but no smile lit up her bony face. Idris took the orange, pulled out his knife and peeled it carefully. Then he passed the segments one by one to the old woman, as if he had simply been doing what she expected of him. She accepted the first two segments, but refused the rest with a gesture that indicated they were for him.

An hour later the bus made a stop at the edge of a eucalyptus wood, a few kilometers from Aïn-Sefra. Once outside, the passengers dispersed, spontaneously forming two groups; on one side the women and children, on the other the men and adolescents. Idris instinctively moved toward the little circle where the men were talking and laughing excitedly and seemed to be observing him.

"Here he is," said an adolescent his own age. "Here comes old Lala Ramirez's friend."

And they all laughed even more. Idris joined them with a questioning look.

"You ought to take precautions, you know, she doesn't have *baraka*, that's the least that can be said!"

"It's especially the people close to her who don't have *baraka*. But she does look after them later, when they're dead."

"Who is Lala Ramirez?" Idris asked.

"That old witch who's been looking at you so lovingly . . ."

"With her evil eye!"

". . . And giving you oranges."

Finally, through all the jokes and allusions, Idris discovered the old woman's story. First, that she had once been very rich, and that she must still be fairly well off, even though she looked like a pauper. Next, that she originally came from the south—an indeterminate south—and had turned the head of a building contractor from Oran who was of Spanish origin and had been living in Béchar while the modern town was being built. He had taken her back to Oran and married her according to the Christian rites and the couple, soon surrounded by six children, had constantly been going back and forth between the two towns. Lala still made this two-way journey, but alone now for several years. In fact, ill fate had dogged this family, carrying off first the husband and then the six children one after another, and finally two babies who had contrived to get born in the middle of the calamities. Everything came into the story, illnesses, murders, accidents, suicides, and the only one left standing, the center of nine graves scattered over several cemeteries, was this antiquated old woman. The reason for her constant travels was to visit her dead, and she was known and feared in every station and on every bus route she used.

"So now you've been warned!"

"I'll be surprised if he stays with her."

"But maybe he doesn't value his life?"

"Or maybe he's attracted by the dead?"

"No, no, that's an old woman's passion, not a young man's!"

The driver sounded his horn to announce their departure. Everyone tried to reconstitute his individual hole. Idris went back to his place on Lala Ramirez's left. He knew who she was now, and curiously enough, she too seemed to be looking at him with increased familiarity. A little later, when all the people around them were eating their snacks, she brought out an oblong packet wrapped in newspaper from under her seat and offered it to Idris in silence. It was a section of a long loaf, with a merguez stuck inside it. Idris hesitated for a moment, and then ate it with relish under the unwavering gaze of the old woman. What did she want of him?

A second orange appeared out of her sleeve as if by magic, and my goodness, after the merguez-bread it couldn't be refused. After that, Idris leaned back in his seat and observed the metamorphosis of the countryside. It was no longer the desert —far from it. Not only was the plain dotted with clumps of acacias, but big farms were succeeded by cultivated fields and crops of vegetables, and the bus was always having to slow down and sound its horn in order to pass tractors and agricultural machines. They crossed a plain covered with cereal crops whose abundance amazed him. And finally, on the outskirts of Oran, the first workers' flats appeared, festooned with lines of multicolored wash drying on their balconies. Now and then groups of children, disturbed in their games, began to run, shrieking, in mad pursuit of the bus. They drove past the administrative center, then past the new mosque, then along the Maata Mohammed El Habib Boulevard, ending up in the

Place du 1er Novembre. Idris turned his head toward his neighbor. Her reptilian gaze was focused on him, and for the first time the shadow of a smile seemed to play about her lips. Making a lot of noise, the people shook themselves and began to push and shove toward the door. As he got out, Idris was struck by the freshness of the air. A uniformly gray sky stretched over the blocks of flats, bristling with television antennas, that seemed gigantic to him. So this was the north, was it? A handful of pale boys were amusing themselves kicking a ball against a dilapidated wall, and each impact sounded like a punch in the face. There was a brutality in the atmosphere, a desolation, an energy that both wounded and swelled the heart. The bus driver, perched up on the roof rack, passed the bundles and suitcases down to some young men, who lined them up along the pavement. Idris had the address of a hostel for emigrants and a letter of recommendation to one of its employees. He was lingering to watch the spectacle of this great city, so new to him, when he heard a murmur in his ear:

"Ismaïl, get a taxi and take me to the Spanish cemetery."

It was old Lala. At the same time she was holding out a fifty-dinar note, folded in four. Attracted by the arrival of the bus, a taxi rank had formed. Made docile by the strangeness of his surroundings, Idris threw himself into the nearest one, followed by Lala. She gave the address: the Saint Louis Church cemetery. But why had she called him Ismaïl? They stopped in front of the church; it had been deconsecrated for several years but its cemetery was still well kept. Lala seemed transformed.

"This is the church of Cardinal Ximenes de Cisneros, the Grand Inquisitor under the Emperor Charles V. You can still see his coat of arms at the entrance to the choir," she explained, in a surprising access of loquacity.

Then she led Idris to the funerary chapels and grandiloquent baroque monuments created by Spanish necrophilia. They stopped in front of a black marble obelisk on whose base, clumsily framed in gold, were a name and a photo: "Ismaïl Ramirez 1940–1957." Idris leaned over the big chains surrounding a rectangle of gray gravel to observe the portrait. It was a boy his own age, as dark as he, whose thin face expressed an uneasy expectation, a vulnerable tenderness, an apparent weakness which in reality was capable of every kind of resistance. Did he really resemble him? Idris was in no position to judge, as he had only a vague idea of his own face. But Lala seemed to be possessed by unshakable certainty. Her longsighted gaze traveled over the descending terraces and cupolas of the old town and, farther away, to the port with its broken-backed cranes, its docks, the freighters at anchor, whose lights were beginning to shine through the twilight.

"Ismaïl, it's you!" she said to Idris, placing her hand on his shoulder. "I've found you at last. You're going to stay with me. Forever. I'm on my own, but I'm rich. I'm adopting you. From now on your name is Ismaïl Ramirez."

Idris looked at her, silently shaking his head. But the old woman refused to see this. She was now staring at one of the blocks of flats half hidden in the evening mist.

"You see that house?" she went on, with a gesture of her chin toward the town. "It belongs to me. It has eleven rooms, three terraces, a patio with a fig tree, kitchens in the basement, and even a Christian chapel. I shall have it all reopened, cleaned, renovated, for you, Ismaïl, and we shall celebrate your return by going and announcing the great news to all the dead of the family. Who knows whether they too won't come back?"

Idris was still saying no with his head. The old woman's madness, and her determination to try to envelop him in the skin of a dead boy, frightened him and made him feel sick. He shrugged off the clawlike hand weighing down his shoulder and took a step backward.

"I'm not Ismaïl. I'm Idris. The day after tomorrow I'm leaving to work in France. Later, I'll come back, later maybe, later . . ."

He was thinking about the photo the Land-Rover woman had taken, but he was careful not to make any allusion to it.

Ismaïl's photo was quite enough for today! Still retreating, he repeated, in the way one calms a child or a terrified animal:

"Later . . . maybe . . . later . . ."

Then he fled and, turning his back on the cemetery, went in search of the hostel whose address he had been given.

THE CAR FERRY, the *Tipasa*, left the next day at ten in the morning and was due to arrive in Marseille the day after that at six in the evening. Idris had some hours ahead of him, but he had to go and get his passport at the ONAMO.[1] office. He stood in line for two hours, only to hear that he needed two identity photos to complete his papers. He was told of an automatic booth where for one dinar he would be able to get the necessary photos. For a long time he searched the unknown streets for the equally unknown object. He found it under the porch of a building where some ironmongers were selling kitchen utensils from trestle tables. The ramshackle booth was occupied by a couple of boys jostling each other and making faces at the camera. They finally left, and Idris took their place behind the curtain. There were flashes. He went out and examined the drawer the prints fall into. There was a photo already in it: that of one of the boys squinting and sticking out his tongue. Idris waited a little longer. Two new images fell: those of a bearded man. He studied himself at length in the cracked mirror in the booth. After all, why wouldn't he have had a beard before he left Tabelbala? Bearded people also have a right to a passport.

He still had an important discovery to make. He turned his steps toward the sea. He had heard people describing beaches covered with blond sand with limpid waves crashing in on them. He had the impression that the sea resembled the sand dunes he had already known in Tabelbala, but whose golden sweep he had particularly noticed in Beni-Abbès. He began to

[1] Up till 1973, the Office National Algérien de la Main-d'Oeuvre dispatched an average of 30,000 Algerian workers a year to France.

walk more quickly, and went down Rue Rahmani Khaled toward the port, where he could already see the varnished masts of the yachts. The ebbing tide had left part of the quay exposed; it seemed to be covered with black, sticky moss. Idris sat down on the stone, his feet on a level with the gritty water in which straws and plastic bottles were floating. So that was it! The nearest yachts were sleeping motionless on mottled water. Farther off, the sea, dotted with boats at anchor, extended to the horizon, where it merged into the equally gray, leaden sky. Idris took a long look at this sad, disappointing sight. At the same time he was discovering a new vision of his native land. For the first time he thought of Tabelbala as a coherent, definable entity. Yes, distance had finally brought together in his memory his mother and his herd, his house and the palm grove, the market square where Salah Brahim parked his bus, the faces of his brothers and his girl cousins. A harsh sob choked in his throat. He felt lost, abandoned, rejected, facing this water, as gray as the beyond. "Ismaïl Ramirez," he murmured under his breath. Had not old Lala, the guardian of the dead, assigned him a place in this funereal city? Tomorrow he was going to embark on the enormous car ferry for a mysterious destination. Was it to escape from life or to be swallowed up in infinity? He slid his index finger into his shirt collar and pulled out his necklace. The golden droplet appeared, warm and soft. He held it up in front of his face, swinging it against the background of the leaden sea. In his memory he could hear Zett Zobeida's mysterious song:

> *The dragonfly flutters low over the water*
> *The cricket creaks on the stone*
> *The dragonfly phrases the tricks of death*
> *The cricket writes the secrets of life*

A little wave came and broke against the quay, splashing him from head to foot. He put his hand to his mouth. On that point, at least, he had not been misled: the water was salty. Salty, undrinkable, sterile.

THE SIGHT of the motorcycles, cars, and trucks being engulfed in the gaping belly of the ferry always attracted the same crowd of idlers and adolescents. The trailer trucks in particular, because of their length and their difficulty in reversing, had to perform laborious maneuvers. But the ship's hold seemed endowed with an unlimited capacity. Sandwiched among the trucks were tourists' cars, and all-terrain vehicles similar to that of the blonde woman. The rubbernecks laughed both pityingly and sympathetically when a patched-up Citroën 2CV began to bounce up and down as it tried to find its place among the mastodons. The drivers and their passengers didn't appear outside again; there were stairs from the car deck giving them access to the upper decks. At last the line of foot passengers was allowed onto the gangway. They were all supposed to have their tickets and passports in their hands, the passport opened to show its photograph. The official didn't even notice the strange dissimilarity between Idris and the bearded man whose portrait was clipped to his passport. Idris cast a brief glance at the rows of reclining seats in the economy-class "sleeping cabins," and then, with the other passengers, crossed the prayer room and the self-service restaurant and came out onto the afterdeck overlooking the quay. There, a dense, colorful crowd was in perpetual motion. The families on land were making eloquent gestures and shouting up to "their" passenger without the slightest chance of making themselves heard. A strange, fanciful communications network was vainly trying to establish itself between the people on the quay and those on board. Abruptly, the deck began to vibrate. The water astern began to seethe. Any minute now Idris would be leaving the African continent for the first time. He was suddenly addressed by an adolescent whose smooth, gentle face was disfigured by a kind of joyous fury.

"I can see *you* haven't got anyone on the quay! Just like me: no one. Yes, that's the way we leave: absolutely alone. That's a real departure. No handkerchiefs, no waving hands. Nothing!"

He was interrupted by a terrific blast from the siren, which startled a flock of sea gulls into taking wing over the port. Slowly, the *Tipasa* pulled away from the quay.

"Look at the quay shoving off!" went on the adolescent, who was getting more and more excited. "That's the way I like Africa: when I see it shoving off behind a boat. Bloody Africa! Two years! Two years of military service! Two years of agony breaking stones in the desert! Me, you know, I've got a trade, I'm a goldsmith. For five generations, from father to son, we've specialized in earrings. Look at my hands. They're the hands of a goldsmith, not the hands of a stone breaker. Bloody Africa! Where're you going, then?"

"Me? To Marseille first. And then I hope to Paris. I've got a cousin there."

"Marseille, Paris—they're not far enough. Not far enough away from the stones in the desert. Talk to me of Brussels, Amsterdam, London, Stockholm. I'm a goldsmith, d'you hear me?"

He said no more. Silence reigned on the deck. Everyone was watching Oran disappearing, the town, the harbor, the ships at anchor, an enormous red-and-green buoy, like a top that belonged to some gigantic child, dancing on its belly, and, in the distance, the hill that dominates the city, the Djebel Murdjajo, crowned by a Spanish fort flying the Algerian Army flag.

Idris, with several others, penetrated into the inner labyrinths of the ship. The passageways, stairways, shopping arcades, and bars constituted a small floating town pervaded by the perpetual throbbing of the engines. Families clustered together and colonized one corner of a saloon or a whole row of seats with their bundles and suitcases. Some were already unpacking their provisions, and a steward took authoritative action to make a woman put out a little gas stove she wanted to cook on. Although it was still early, the truck drivers had already got together in the bar around a noisy, jovial table, and were beginning to get down to some serious drinking. The division of the passengers into two categories—those who had money to spend and those who hadn't—was already established. As for the superior category, the first-class passengers in their private cabins with portholes and a dining room with white-clothed tables, they remained invisible and inaccessible, entrenched behind the locked doors of one of the upper forward decks.

A very slight pitching indicated that the boat had just reached the open sea when the call of the muezzin came through the loudspeakers and invited the faithful to come to the prayer room, where the mats had already been unrolled for the third salat. Idris, who like most of the young of his generation was very little inclined to religious practices, observed the crowd from a distance, bowing and prostrating themselves. When they dispersed, he was surprised to see that the goldsmith had been among them and was coming over to him.

"Don't you respect the traditions of Islam?" he asked.

"Not all of them," Idris answered crossly.

"I hope for your sake that you will come around to them. Where we're going, religion is more necessary than it is at home. You're going to find yourself surrounded by foreigners, by people who don't care, by enemies. You may find that your only defense against despair and poverty will be the Koran and the mosque."

"But just now you were cursing your own country."

The goldsmith said nothing for a moment, and watched the turbulent surface of the sea.

"The trouble is, you know, that many of us can live neither in our own country nor abroad."

"What have they got left, then?"

"Misfortune."

"I could have stayed in Tabelbala if I'd wanted to. In Tabelbala we haven't got anything, but we aren't short of anything. That's the way it is in an oasis."

"Then why did you leave?"

"Just for the sake of leaving. There are two kinds of people where I come from, and you can sometimes find them in the same family: the ones who stay where they were born and the ones who need to leave. I'm one of the second sort. I had to leave. And then, I'd been photographed by a blonde woman. She went back to France with my photo."

"So you left home to go and find your photo?"

The goldsmith gave him a mocking look.

"To go and find my photo? No, not exactly. It's something else. It's probably better to say: to go and be with my photo."

"Well, well! But you're a great thinker, you are! Your photo is in France, and it attracts you like a magnet attracts a piece of iron."

"Not only in France. I've already found my photo in Beni-Abbès, in Béchar, and in Oran."

"You find pieces of it along your way and you stick it together?"

"Yes, if you like. So far, though, the pieces I've found aren't at all like me. Here, just look at this, for example."

He showed him his passport, opened at the page with the bearded man. The goldsmith looked at him with a worried air.

"You could get into trouble. Maybe you ought to grow a beard."

"That would be worse, I hardly have one. And anyway, it isn't up to me to look like my photo. It's my photo that ought to look like me, isn't it?"

"Do you really believe that? But your experience already proves that it's the other way around. An image is possessed of a force for evil. It isn't the faithful, devoted servant you'd like it to be. It takes on all the appearances of a servant, yes, but in actual fact it's crafty, lying, and imperious. Out of the depths of its evil nature it does all it can to reduce you to slavery. That too is in religion."

[88]

Idris listened to him without really understanding. And yet the misadventures he had suffered ever since his meeting with the blonde woman shed a curious light on what the goldsmith had been saying.

At noon the goldsmith took him into the self-service restaurant, and Idris was torn between hunger and the embarrassment he felt at accepting the invitation of his somewhat disturbing elder. They shared a table with a truck driver, a blond giant with china-blue eyes whose enormous arms were covered with indecent tattoos. He taunted the two young Maghrebis, and took it into his head to make them drink some red wine. The goldsmith rose to the occasion with alacrity, and surprised Idris by downing glass after glass with the man, in spite of the interdict of the Islamic religion. He laughed at the driver's jokes in all the right places, answered them with jokes of his own, and wanting to draw Idris into the conversation he began to talk French to him, whereas before they had talked only in Berber. In actual fact the goldsmith's duplicity was admirable, and Idris wondered whether he would ever manage to get on such familiar terms with the French. The driver bought them coffee, and then retired to his second-class cabin for a siesta; it was well deserved, he told them, after ten hours' night driving along the Maghreb coast road.

As night was falling, a rumor spread among the passengers and drew them out onto the decks and passageways on the port side. The ship was sailing along the coast of Ibiza, where a few lights were beginning to flicker. Later it was almost dark when people began to point out the lights of Majorca, the largest of the Balearic Islands, to starboard. After that, the boat plunged into a sea of unfathomable darkness.

Idris was asleep in a chair, lulled by a swell that was becoming heavier and heavier. He was woken by the groans of a woman sitting near him. Her head was rolling from right to left and a froth was bubbling on her lips. Finally she stood up, took a couple of steps, and collapsed on the floor. There, crouching on all fours, she began to vomit, in deep-drawn, noisy hiccups.

"A woman being seasick has no more sense of shame than one giving birth."

This was the goldsmith. Behind him, the truck driver was walking with a rolling gait and guffawing.

"That cabin without a porthole, it's just not possible," the driver said. "You're boxed in like you were in a coffin. Well, then, kids, if you want my bunk, you're welcome to it. I'd rather have a seat."

"Coming?" said the goldsmith.

Idris stood up and followed him.

"You can have a shower too!" the driver called after them.

And it was true that at this hour of the night there was something sepulchral about the cabin. No opening onto the outside world. Two metal bunks fixed to the steel walls. Three people sleeping the sleep of the dead. A minute shower stall. And above all this, in the humid, vibrating atmosphere, the glaucous glimmer of a night-light. The door shut heavily behind the two adolescents. They hesitated for a moment, and then the goldsmith began to undress. Naked, he went into the shower. Idris followed suit. The only way they could both squeeze onto the shower tray was by clinging to one another. The same applied to the one free bunk, where they lay down, still dripping wet. The relief he felt at this close contact with his companion made Idris aware of the terrible solitude he had been suffering, body and soul, since he had left his family. Maternal tenderness and the eroticism of lovers are only particular aspects of the ardent need of physical contact that is the essence of the flesh and the heart. In this semi-obscurity, with his eyes closed, and lulled by the swell and the muffled roar of the engines, he remembered his friend Ibrahim, who had disappeared into the entrails of the Hassi el Hora well. He was drifting off to sleep when the goldsmith disentangled himself and, propping himself up on one elbow, held up Idris's golden droplet in the narrow pencil of light.

"What's this?"

"It's my Saharan grigri."

"But it's gold!"

"Maybe . . ."

The goldsmith rotated the pear-shaped object in the light, and frowned.

"Whoever gave it to you wasn't joking."

"No one gave it to me."

"Bulla aurea."

"What?"

"That's Latin: *bulla aurea,* the golden bubble. Every goldsmith knows it. It's a Roman, or even Etruscan, emblem that still exists in some Saharan tribes. Freeborn Roman children wore this golden droplet around their necks hanging on a special ring, as proof of their condition. When they exchanged their child's toga for the virile toga they also abandoned the *bulla aurea* and gave it as an offering to the household gods."

"What a lot you know!"

"The goldsmith's trade isn't only a craft, it's also a traditional culture. I could tell you about fibulae, peltae, Solomon's seals, Hands of Fatma," he added, lying down again.

"Well, then, my golden droplet, what does it mean?"

"That you're a freeborn child."

"And then?"

"And then . . . You'll become a man, and then you'll see what will happen to your golden droplet, and to you too . . ."

IT MUST HAVE BEEN about midday the next day when the whole ship heard an announcement that brought the passengers flocking into the restaurant: the TV! There were three sets on which a flickering image suddenly appeared, disappeared, and then came back again, jumping up and down feverishly. The first image came live from France! A crowd of apprehensive, attentive immigrants, bony-faced, somber-eyed, awaited this first message from the Promised Land. The screens quivered, went dead, then lit up again; a landscape, a silhouette, a face, undulated and then became stabilized. A couple were walking in a meadow. They were young, good-looking, in love. They were smiling at each other. Two radiant children rushed up to them through the grass and flowers. Long embrace. Bliss. Suddenly the image became immobilized. A serious-looking man in glasses was superimposed. On a level with his face, his hand was holding a life insurance contract. Next came a picture of an attractive house in Provence. Breakfasting by the swimming pool, the whole family was laughing. Bliss. This time it was thanks to the washing powder Soleil. It was raining. An elegant woman was walking, protected by her umbrella. Passing in front of a shopwindow she thought herself so chic that she smiled at herself. How bright and shining her teeth were! Bliss. You must use Briodent toothpaste. The small screens went dark. That was all. The men and women traveling in economy class looked at one another. So that's France? They exchanged their impressions. But then everyone fell silent, because the image was back. A voice explained that students had been demonstrating in the Latin Quarter and the riot squad had used tear gas against them. The policemen, helmeted, masked, and equipped with Plexiglas shields, looked like Japanese samurai from the Middle Ages. The students threw stones at them, then ran away and dispersed. Flares burst in their midst. A close-up showed a very young girl's face streaming with blood. Once again the screens went dead.

Two hours later the French coast was within sight. The families began to collect their children and baggage. Idris found himself leaning over the rail beside the goldsmith, watching the Château d'If go by. For the benefit of the first-class tourists, no doubt, the loudspeakers began to bawl out that this was the fortress in which the Man in the Iron Mask, who was perhaps the twin brother of Louis XIV, had been imprisoned, as had the Count of Monte Cristo and the Abbé Faria, Alexandre

Dumas's famous characters. The crowd of Maghrebis received this information with all the respect of perfect incomprehension.

"I've got a job in an illegal jewelry workshop in Paris," the goldsmith said. "And Étienne, the truck driver, is going to give me a lift there. I don't know when we'll meet again. There's just one thing I wanted to tell you. You know I'm a goldsmith: a smith is 'someone who shapes metal by hammering.' But goldsmiths abandoned gold a long time ago; nowadays we only work in silver. Our bracelets, our trays, our cassolettes, everything we make is made in silver. Why? Because most of us refuse to work in gold these days. The truth is that we don't know the special technique needed to work in gold. But there's something else. We believe that gold brings bad luck. Silver is pure, straightforward, honest. Gold is much too precious, it excites greed and provokes theft, violence, crime. I'm telling you this because I see you going off into the unknown with your *bulla aurea*. It's a symbol of freedom, but its metal has become disastrous. May God keep you!"

Thirteen

IDRIS DID IN FACT lose sight of the goldsmith in the crowd milling around the customs men's windows. In comparison with the families encumbered with children and luggage his case seemed to be of extreme simplicity, and in spite of his passport photo he was one of the first to reach the harbor station.

So he was in France. He explored the ground with his feet, to feel its consistency. He opened his eyes wide to take in the obvious differences that ought to have distinguished Marseille from Oran. And what did he see? A little more animation, a little more color, more life, a more expansive mood than in Oran. Marseille was a town of the south, Oran a town of the north. But all things considered, he was disappointed to feel so little out of his element on this opposite shore of the Mediterranean. The shock occurred a little later, though, when he came upon a huge poster adorning the walls of the car ferry reservation offices:

TAKE YOUR CAR
AND SPEND YOUR XMAS HOLIDAYS
IN THE PARADISE OF A SAHARAN OASIS

Dumbfounded, Idris looked at the proffered image of a Saharan oasis. A clump of palm trees and extravagant flowers surrounded a kidney-shaped swimming pool. Blond girls in skimpy bikinis were smirking around the turquoise pool, drinking from tall glasses out of angled straws. Two tame gazelles were inclining their elegant heads over a huge basket filled with oranges, grapefruit, and pineapples. A Saharan oasis? Wasn't Tabelbala a Saharan oasis? And wasn't he, Idris, the pure product of that oasis? He couldn't recognize himself in that dream image. But had he recognized himself in Salah Brahim's photo of a donkey, and hadn't an unknown man even insinuated himself into his passport? He shivered in the freshening air; night seemed to fall more quickly here than in Africa. In his pocket was a crumpled piece of paper, the page torn out of the Mozabite's notebook with the address of a hotel and a few words of recommendation: Hôtel Radio, 10 Rue Parmentier. He questioned a passerby. Gesture of helplessness. He should go to the Place Jules-Guesde. Someone there would be sure to know. He started walking down the Boulevard de Paris, constantly having to jump out of the way of the big trucks hurtling down from the Gare d'Arenc. The Place Jules-Guesde looked as if it had been devastated by a recent bombardment. In the middle of an expanse of waste ground surrounded by crumbling walls there was a kind of triumphal archway. Idris crossed this piece of desert and came to the Rue Bernard-Dubois, where he found himself back in Africa. There were nothing but Turkish baths, Islamic bookshops, North African secondhand-clothes dealers, small restaurants at whose doors sheep's heads dripping with grease were revolving on electric spits. The Impasse Tancrède-Martel, a street consisting entirely of steps, was colonized by fortune-tellers and public letter-writers, the latter selling Korans and devotional books. The entire district was no more than a network of back streets—Rue des Petites-Maries, du Baignoir, du Tapis-Vert, Longue-des-Capucins—smelling of curry, incense, and urine, in which he finally found the Rue Parmentier and the Hôtel Radio. Even though it was still early, he had to knock for a long time before the door was opened. The proprietor, Youssef Baghabagha, let him in suspiciously. The hotel was full. He wasn't taking any more guests. Even so, he deciphered the Mozabite merchant's recommendation and immediately became more hospitable. There actually was a vacant room, but you had to pay in advance—ten francs a night —and the hotel closed at eleven.

The bed was big and immaculate, but the window looked out onto a dark courtyard, so that both day and night you had to put on the hanging ceiling light, which had a fluted glass shade. Idris lay down on the bedcover and immediately fell asleep. At Tabelbala, dawn was breaking. He ought to have been getting up and rounding up his herd, but he was delighting in his idleness and refused to open his eyes. He could hear his mother coming and going as she prepared the beta, the morning soup made of bran, pimentos, and onions. One of the ewes in the compound was bleating with abnormal insistence. Had she been injured? He must go and see. Idris was amazed that his mother, who must have heard the animal's cries, hadn't already come and dragged him out of bed. Another pitiful bleat. Come on—get up! Idris shook himself. He wasn't in Tabelbala, blessed by the rising sun. He was in an unknown room, in an unknown town, in an unknown country. An anguished sob escaped him. He must go home! He must undertake, in reverse, the tremendous journey that had finally jettisoned him on this bed! At this moment he heard a ewe bleating in the courtyard. On this point at least his dream had not deceived him. He felt suddenly comforted by this familiar presence. There was a live sheep under his window. Perhaps it was going to be ritually sacrificed at the end of the week? He got up, went down the stairs and out of the hotel. Night had fallen, and the street, though dark during the day, was ablaze with all the lights of its shopwindows, street signs, and illuminated advertisements. The Rue Parmentier leads to the Rue des Convalescents, which comes out at the Boulevard d'Athènes. Here there were great festivities. Fairground booths, shooting galleries, lotteries, Aunt Sallies, cluttered the pavements. Cafés with wide-open doors looked like golden caverns, magnified by immense mirrors; in the back glowed the green light of the billiard tables around which men in shirt sleeves were officiating. Above the entrance to a movie theater an enormous couple lay in each other's arms according to the rules of the art—the woman underneath, the man on top— with tragic gazes and mouths glued together. But Idris was dying of hunger, and he was attracted by the Pantagruelic menu at a McDonald's: Hamburger, Cheeseburger, Filet-o-Fish, Big Mac, Apple Danish, Vanilla, Strawberry, Chocolate Shakes. All these were far too expensive for him, but he actually felt too poverty-stricken to resist. Prodigality is the one luxury of the poor. He treated himself to a solitary blowout to appease his anguish, to celebrate his arrival in France, and also quite simply because he was hungry.

He had been warned that on the other side of the sea you found a country where it was cold and foggy. It was raining lightly when he left the McDonald's. And yet the booths were doing a roaring trade. Senegalese smothered in costume jewelry, Moroccans carrying rugs over one shoulder, veiled women, barefoot in their sandals, walking with swaying steps, maintained the African atmosphere in spite of the drizzle. Attracted by the sense of intimacy in the alleyways, Idris turned into the Rue Thubaneau. Stationed at the curb, or nonchalantly leaning against the door of a sleazy hotel, Ghanaian streetwalkers, as black as night and harnessed like circus horses, watched him go by, puffing at their long cigarette holders. He barely gave them a glance. A drunk, suddenly emerging from a noisy, smoke-filled café, grabbed him by the arm and tried to pull him inside. Idris shook him off. He stopped only when he saw a very different girl from the others, who was making up her face using the window of a dress shop as a mirror. She was a long-haired blonde. She resembled the woman in the Land-Rover, in spite of her miniskirt, her tall black boots, and the fishnet stockings clinging to her enormous thighs. She must have seen him in the glass, as she turned around and addressed him.

"Hallo, deary! Looks like you go for blondes! Don't be scared, come over here."

Idris went up to her.

"Oh my, he's young, he's very young. What's more, he's just this minute arrived from the sticks, that's for sure. Isn't that right, deary! We still smell of the hot Sahara sand!"

Idris was dazzled by the girl's fat, naked shoulders. The Land-Rover woman had been wearing a top that gave her a vaguely masculine air. He raised a timid hand to touch this milk-white, perfumed flesh.

"Now, now, hands off, deary! Because I wouldn't be surprised if you were the broke type. Show us your wallet."

Idris lowered his arm, not understanding.

"Oh, come on, your papers—shit!"

This time he understood. It was the supreme commandment. Obediently, he took out his wallet and gave it to the woman. She glanced at it briefly and gave it back to him.

"Just as I thought. Nothing, or as good as. Hey, though, that thing around your neck doesn't look bad. Let me look."

She had caught a glimpse of the golden droplet around Idris's neck. He made a feeble gesture to defend it, but she pulled his necklace off with all the dexterity of a monkey and held it up to the light.

"Hell, it's fabulous! Looks like solid gold. I wonder where you nicked it."

She put the necklace around her neck and, to judge its effect, turned to the shopwindow. Then, obeying a reflex provoked by the mirror, she opened her handbag and went on with her makeup. Idris watched her applying a purplish-red lipstick, then screwing up her mouth in every direction to spread the color. Next she began to groom her false eyelashes with a tiny black brush. While she was dabbing at her cheeks, Idris thought back to his mother sitting in front of old Kuka. With a woolen brush dipped in saffron, Kuka traced the ritual signs on his mother's face. The yellow dye stood out starkly against her dark skin: on her forehead two broad horizontal lines parallel to her eyebrows, two strokes at the root of her nose, a broad vertical line starting from the middle of her lower lip and going down to the tip of her chin, and, most importantly, under both her eyes a patch from which three vertical barbs descended, like traces of copious tears. Such indeed is the painted mask of the married woman in Tabelbala. It was not a question, as it was here, of intensifying the bleeding cushion of the lips or the sooty blackness of the orbits, but of positioning signs that belonged to an age-old tradition which everyone could read.

"Well, how do I look? Do you like me?"

The girl had turned around and was looking at Idris. He held out a hand to her neck to take his golden droplet back. The girl brushed this timid hand aside. Then, smiling at him, she unbuttoned her blouse and revealed her breasts. Idris's hands stretched up to this display of pulpy flesh. The girl stopped smiling, abruptly did up her blouse, and led Idris over to the staircase of a building on the other side of the road.

When he knocked at the door of the Hôtel Radio, it was long past its closing time. Idris spent the rest of the night curled up on a bench in the Cours Belsunce.

Fourteen

THE PARIS TRAIN left at 11:48. From early morning Idris had been wandering about in the Gare Saint-Charles. Its turbulent atmosphere intoxicated him pleasantly. In his distress, he felt comforted by the farewells and meetings which accompanied the departure and arrival of every train and in which he participated as a hungry witness. He called on his slender knowledge of geography to try to imagine the destinations of the trains he saw leaving for Genoa, Toulouse, or Clermont-Ferrand. He tried to establish a link between these towns and the railway posters, which showed Mont Saint-Michel, Azay-le-Rideau, Versailles, or the Pointe du Raz. Why did these places that were so important in French imagery never correspond to the great cities the trains went to, or to the workers they carried? Here, it seemed, were two totally unrelated worlds: on the one hand a reality that was accessible, but rough and gray, and on the other hand a fairyland that was gentle and colorful, but situated somewhere remote and intangible.

At eleven, the Paris train arrived at the platform. Idris waited to board it until quite a few passengers had taken their places. Observe, imitate, do what the others did so as not to betray his barbarity in the middle of these civilized people. He found a corner seat on the corridor side, a place that enables you to get into and out of the compartment without disturbing anyone. A young man who had come rushing in at the last moment apparently had no such scruples. He trod on a few feet as he made his way over to the window, which he lowered, and then began chatting gaily with some other young men who had remained on the platform. When the train began to pull out there were loud shouts, joined hands, and sweeping gestures. Then the young man, his face still lit up by these farewells, flopped down on the free seat opposite Idris. Still smiling, he looked at him without seeing him. Idris devoured him with his eyes. How deeply rooted in his country, how sure of himself, how well adapted this young Frenchman his own age seemed! When the train later stopped at Arles, he went back to the window and leaned out over the platform, as if he was expecting to find his friends there too. Idris shut his eyes and abandoned himself to the regular, soothing rhythm of the moving train. Once again he heard Zett Zobeida's music. Once again he saw the black-and-red woman, surrounded by the musicians with their enigmatic ritornello:

> The dragonfly flutters low over the water
> The cricket creaks on the stone
> The dragonfly phrases the tricks of death
> The cricket writes the secret of life.

The dance was interrupted when the train stopped at Avignon, but then it began again:

> The dragonfly's wing is a skit
> The cricket's wing is a script.

Idris saw the golden droplet twisting around on the dancer's neck, and then swinging in the sun at the end of its broken thong. He heard the Marseille prostitute: "Hell, it's fabulous! Looks like solid gold." Between the girl's open thighs her pubic triangle was dark brown, because her platinum-blonde hair was of course dyed. Idris had lost his *bulla aurea*, the oasis talisman, the sign of freedom. Now, to the rhythm of the train, he was hurtling toward the country of images. They were approaching Valence when he shook himself, left the compartment, and went and leaned against the rail over the corridor window. They were passing the dry Provençal scrublands, with their olive groves and lavender fields. The young man came and stood beside him. He gave Idris a friendly glance and then began to talk as if to himself, but gradually addressing Idris more directly.

"We're still in Provence. Cypress trees planted in rows to protect the crops from the mistral. Roman tiles on the roofs. But not for much longer now. Valence is the frontier with the Midi. There the climate changes, the landscape changes, the buildings change."

"But it's still France?" Idris asked.

"It isn't the same France, it's the North, it's more my kind of France."

He spoke about himself. His name was Philippe. His family owned an estate in Picardy, near Amiens, where he was born. He had been brought up in Paris.

"The Midi, for me, means holidays. It's also a kind of curiosity, a kind of folklore, with its accent, and the stories they tell in Marseille. But I can understand that someone from Provence feels a bit as if he's in exile when he crosses the frontier at Valence. It's gray and cold. The people talk with a northern accent."

"With a northern accent?"

"Yes, an accent that isn't Provençal, the accent you hear in Lyon or Paris for example. You see, for the people of the South, the people of the South don't have an accent. They reckon they speak normally. It's the rest of the French who have an accent, 'l'assente poinntu.' For the people in the North, it's the Meridionals who have an accent. They find it amusing and attractive, but they don't take it seriously. It's Marius's accent."

"And the people from North Africa?"

"The *pieds-noirs?* Oh, them, they're even worse: they speak what we call 'le pataouet.' That's the absolute end. It isn't even proper French."

"No, I'm not talking about the *pieds-noirs.* I mean the Arabs, the Berbers?"

"Well, them, that's not the same thing. They're foreigners. They have their own language, Arabic or Berber. They have to learn French. You—what are you?"

"A Berber."

"Then you're really in a foreign country here."

"Less than in Germany, even so, or in England. In Algeria, we've always seen the French."

"Yes, we know each other. Every Frenchman has his own idea about Algeria and the Sahara, even if he's never set foot there. They're part of our dreams."

"I had my photo taken by a Frenchwoman."

"Was it a good photo?"

"I don't know. I haven't seen it yet. But since I left my country I've been getting more and more afraid that it won't be a good photo. Well—not exactly the photo I was expecting."

"I always take heaps of photos with me when I travel," said Philippe. "They keep me company. They reassure me."

He led Idris back into the compartment and took a small album out of his bag.

"Here: this is me with my brothers and sister."

Idris looked at the photo and then at Philippe, as if to compare the two.

"It's you all right, but younger."

"It was two years ago. My brothers are on the right, and my father's behind. The old lady is my grandmother. She died this spring. This is our family house near Amiens with Pipo, the gardener's dog. Those are the garden paths where I learned to walk and ride a bicycle. This is the whole family picnicking in the state forest. My first communion, I'm the third on the left. Ah, and then this one—it's a secret!"

Laughing, he pretended to hide the photo, but finally, serious again, he passed it to Idris.

"That's Fabienne, the woman I'm in love with. We're engaged. Well—not officially. She's studying political science, like me, but she's three years older than I am. Does it show?"

Idris looked at the photo eagerly. He had recognized the typical blonde, like the one in the Land-Rover and the one in Marseille. Then his face clouded over and he gave the album back to Philippe, looking at him suspiciously. Everything this young Frenchman had told him about himself, his family, their house, his country, everything that distinguished him from Idris, had just taken concrete form in the image of this woman. Philippe belonged to the race of blonde women who stole photos and golden droplets. His kindness, his goodwill, the picnic meal he shared with Idris, his running commentaries on the landscape as the train passed through the Vivarais uplands, the gentle foothills of the Beaujolais region, the Champagne plain with its fir plantations—none of this dissipated Idris's agonized certainty that he was entirely surrounded by strangers, and that an obscure danger was lying in wait for him.

When the train arrived in Paris at the Gare de Lyon, Philippe seemed to forget him and to be absorbed in trying to spot his family among the crowd massed on the platform. Idris got out behind him and saw him immediately surrounded by a demonstrative group. He realized that the brief complicity that had brought them together no longer existed. Propelled by the stream of travelers, he reached the pavement outside the station where a long line of taxis was slowly moving up. Night had fallen. The air was limpid but almost cold. The Boulevard Diderot and the whole length of the Rue de Lyon were reduced to scintillating headlights, illuminated signs, shopwindows, café terraces, tricolored traffic lights. Idris hesitated for a moment, and then slowly made his way into this sea of images.

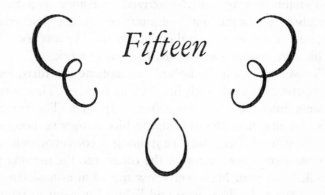

Fifteen

HIS COUSIN ACHOUR, ten years older than Idris, was a big, jovial young man. He had left Tabelbala five years before and—however sporadically—sent optimistic letters and modest money orders back to his family. Mogadem had written to him to recommend his nephew, but Idris had left without waiting for his reply. So he was relieved to find him at the Sonacotra hostel in the Rue Myrha in the XVIIIth arrondissement. He had a small room there in a sort of apartment that contained five other rooms, a shower room, and a communal kitchen with six gas burners and six padlocked refrigerators. In all, the hostel contained twelve bachelor flats, each with six rooms, to which were appended a prayer room and a television room. Achour introduced Idris to the owner of the establishment, a repatriated Algerian *pied-noir* whom everyone called Isidore, as if it were his first name, whereas in fact it was his patronymic. He agreed to allow Idris to share his cousin's room temporarily. Isidore would shut his eyes to this—fairly common—infringement of the police regulations.

Achour made up for his lack of professional qualifications by an apparently inexhaustible ability to turn his hand to any and every task. True, he had done a stint as a semi-skilled worker with Renault shortly after he arrived in France. But he had taken advantage of the first "voluntary redundancy" scheme to leave, and never set foot in the place again. He was not a man who liked regular, monotonous, restricting work.

"The worst thing is the noise," he explained to Idris, recalling this dismal period of his life. "O my brother! The moment you walk into the place your head explodes. The smelting works, for instance: the old engine blocks they've bought as scrap, they send them juddering along a conveyor belt until they crash down one on top of the other into the melting pot. It's hell, I tell you. Me—you know me—I'm a musician, and even a dancer. To do that to me! When I got out in the evening I couldn't hear a thing. I'm quite sure I'd have gone deaf if I'd stayed there. But even worse than that, you know, is their contempt for the man who has to work in that noise. Because the engineers have never taken the trouble to organize the work to make it less noisy. No—that's of no importance! Workmen are wooden-headed! Why bother?"

After that he had been a platform sweeper in the métro, a brief episode of which all he remembered was the famous cleaners' strike which had gone on for four weeks. As the French public utilities are not allowed to employ foreigners, the nine hundred Arabs, Kabyles, and Senegalese working in the métro could only be employed by the Paris transport board through the intermediary of private subcontractors, so their strike hit two employers of equally bad faith. The strikers got together at the Labor Exchange and joined the socialist union, the CFDT, *en bloc*, for which they were rewarded by a friendly visit from Edmond Maire. He was welcomed with youyous and dances, while a young Senegalese, still dancing, offered him a little bunch of roses. His speech was immediately translated into Arab, Berber, and Allcolor.

"But you see, cousin, nothing is ever simple or obvious, because the other union, the CGT, immediately brought the train cleaners out on strike—as a measure of solidarity, so they said. But in actual fact it was a backhanded blow against us, because our demands had nothing in common with those of the train cleaners, and in the end this simply confused the issue."

Idris was listening intently, even though he didn't understand the first thing about the conflicts between CFDT platform cleaners and CGT train cleaners. He felt he was returning to reality when Achour began to describe a frightful December he had spent in Corsica picking clementine oranges. Fourteen hours' work a day, a ghastly bivouac in a shed with some thirty other damned souls like himself—Moroccans for the most part—exploited by their ruthless Corsican employers.

"Ever since that trip, I can't even look at a mandarin orange without taking to my heels. No, you see, cousin, you must never go down to the South of France or to Corsica. In the first place, the winter there is colder than anywhere else. Those December nights in Corsica! I didn't think I'd ever get out of the place alive! And then the people—the darker-skinned they are, the more curly-haired they are, the more like us they are —the more arrogant they are with us. If I was asked one day to go and pick clementines in Sweden or Finland I might give it some thought, but I don't really expect that to happen."

Next he had been a dishwasher in various establishments: day nurseries, milk bars, factory canteens, restaurants, fast-food places, cafeterias, school canteens. The sole charm of these jobs had been their brevity and the kind of lottery by which they were allocated. At the national employment agency, would-be dishwashers were given numbers from 1 to 1,000. As the offers of jobs arrived only in dribs and drabs, you could wait for weeks or even months. True, the waiting time was frequently shortened by the disappearance of the bearer of the number called, either because he had lost heart or because he had found employment elsewhere.

"But *I* was always there when my number came up,"

Achour explained proudly. "In the first place, I enjoy waiting. Waiting for work is the least tiring work I know. And also the least messy. And that's a consideration. I've spent whole days sitting on a bench at the agency listening to them calling out numbers. Often they were so far removed from mine that I could stay away for a few days. That was like a sort of holiday, and during that time the work went on by itself with the numbers being called out. The thing was, though, that you had to be back in time. And for that, I had a kind of flair. I could sense my number coming up. There wasn't a single time when I turned up after they'd called it in my absence. And then there was always the surprise, which was amusing. You never knew whether you were going to land in a Neapolitan pizzeria, a Breton crêperie, or La Tour d'Argent. The only trouble was that you had to eat on the premises. That sounds like a joke, but I swear to you, cousin, that the disadvantage of working in the restaurant trade is the food. In the first place, the time. Because, naturally, it's at mealtimes that you're always working flat out. So you yourself eat at idiotic hours. I could never get used to having supper either at six or at midnight. At six, I'm not hungry. At midnight, I'm nauseated by all the dirty plates and disgusting leavings I've been manipulating for five hours running. In the end, I stopped eating. I lost kilos. It couldn't go on."

He had also groomed dogs and carried a sandwich board. ("For a timid fellow like me it has the advantage that no one notices you. You might even say you become invisible. I mean it! The passersby look at the board you're carrying on your shoulders, but they don't even see you!") He had been a billposter, and he had taken old ladies out for walks. ("There was one really nice one, you know. I used to walk slowly, keeping at her pace, giving her my arm, like a good son, full of respect and all that. And then one day, wham! We're passing the Square de Jessaint, and she says to me, "Let's not go in there, it's full of wogs!" Hadn't she ever looked at me?") He had also been a pyrotechnist ("You can just imagine how many people they need for their fireworks on the thirteenth of July! But, well, that really can be called a seasonal trade!"), a lifeguard in a swimming pool ("I managed for two months not to let on that I couldn't swim. How's that for a record?"), a salesman for Toutou, the food for upper-class dogs ("The boss made us open a can of Toutou in the middle of the shop and eat whole spoonfuls of the stuff in front of the customers with great greedy yum-yums. And after that we were supposed to go and have lunch!"), a window cleaner, a car cleaner, and a cleaner of corpses in the morgue ("It's incredible, all the things I've cleaned in my life! Trouble is, it puts you off cleaning yourself. People who clean anything at all are always as dirty as pigs").

For the moment, he had got himself a job with the XVIIIth arrondissement local council as a temporary street sweeper, and a brief visit to the highways department authorized him to take on his cousin as his assistant. Wearing a municipal cap and a scarlet ribbon across his chest, Idris thus discovered *la vie parisienne* in its most humble aspect. He was befriended by a gray-mustached veteran who was still sweeping because he loved the job and who taught him the art of making a good brush by tying green birch twigs together with a split bramble. As they were a team, they were entrusted with a little cart equipped with a plastic rubbish bag and a dustpan and brush. They not only had to pick up the bits of paper and the dogs' mess on the pavements and clear the gutters, but also had to empty the seventeen public litter bins in the sector they were responsible for. Idris had persuaded Achour to let him have the stopcock key to the gutter hydrants. He liked unleashing the gurgling torrent and watching its flow, continually impeded by the barrages formed by piles of refuse or the tires of parked cars. It reminded him of the work that had to be done to clear and keep the sand out of the irrigation channels in the Tabelbala palm grove which were fed by the fegagirs. Even so, he couldn't get over his amazement at this city, under constant threat of being crushed under the weight of its own dejecta, obsessed by the urgency of the evacuation of its detritus, fighting against the accumulation of all its surpluses, whereas an oasis suffers only from poverty, want, and emptiness.

Achour, between two brush strokes, never lost an opportunity to lecture him on the subject, and to communicate the fruits of his long experience of being an immigrant.

"Here, it isn't the same as in our country," he would say. "In our country you're stuck in a family, in a village. If you marry, good God, you become the property of your mother-in-law! You become something like a bit of furniture that belongs to the house. Here, no, there's freedom. Yes, freedom is great. But just a minute! Freedom is terrible, too! Well then, here, no family, no village, no mother-in-law. You're on your own. With masses of people who pass by without giving you a glance. You can fall down. The passersby won't stop. No one will pick you up. That's what freedom is. It's hard. Very hard."

His young cousin's timidity, his inability to take advantage of the slightest opportunity that came his way, his rather touchy show of pride when anyone seemed to take an interest in him—no, really, he had to change if he wanted to survive in Paris.

"Here, you're like a cork floating on the water," he explained. "The waves toss you to the right, to the left, you sink, you come up again. So you have to take advantage of everything that turns up. For instance, you're young and good-looking. Well then, if someone smiles at you, you mustn't hesitate: go and see what it means. It may be good for you. You mustn't react like a girl. A girl has her reputation to protect, a woman's honor. She mustn't commit herself, or she's lost forever. You're not a girl. You've got nothing to lose. And in any case, we've no right to be choosy."

And of course, there was the environment of the Sonacotra hostel, its owner, Isidore, and the ever-changing throng of the other immigrants. With the residents of the hostel, Isidore, in the heart of Paris, had reconstituted the paternal, tyrannical relations he had had fifteen years earlier with the Arab workmen in the semolina factory he had managed in Batna. "There's nothing I don't know about the wogs," he would assure the inspectors who came to cast a routine glance over the hostel premises. "I know how to talk to them. With me, there's never any trouble." And it was true that the immigrants had no cause for complaint about his guardianship, which, though obviously indiscreet and meddlesome, was, all things considered, efficient.

"The French," Achour commented, "you mustn't think they don't like us. They like us in their own way. But on condition that we keep our place. We have to be humble and inferior. The French won't put up with a rich and powerful Arab. For example, the Gulf emirs, who sell them their oil—they make the French sick! No, an Arab has got to stay poor. The French are charitable toward poor Arabs, especially the left-wing French. And they so enjoy feeling charitable!"

But his point of view was not exempt from severity and demands.

"Even so, there's one thing that all these French people ought to acknowledge. Which is that it's us wogs who've made modern France. Three thousand kilometers of autoroute, the Montparnasse tower, the National Industries and Techniques building, the Marseille métro, and soon Roissy Airport, and later the express métro, the RER—that's us, that's us, that's always us!"

He was discouraged, though, by the passive, dreamy attitude of the majority of the other immigrants.

"Look at the men in the hostel. I sometimes wonder what goes on in their heads. If you talk to them about the future, there are two things they can't accept. The first is the idea of going back home. Oh no, never! They've left it, and for good. Even so, there's some who do think of going back. But only a very, very long time from now when the country has become a sort of paradise on earth. In other words, never. But they aren't happy here either. They can see very well that they aren't wanted. Will they stay here forever, then? Oh no, never! What *do* they want, then? Neither to go home nor to stay in France. One of them said to me the other day, "Here, it's hell, but back home, it's death." What are they dreaming of? They themselves don't know!"

Naturally Idris had told him all about the business of his photo. Achour had listened with a worried air. And he had concluded, gloomily:

"Basically, you see, your blonde with her camera was a trap, an enormous trap. And, my brother, you fell headfirst into that trap. Poor you! Will you be able to get out of it?"

But Idris never told him about Zett Zobeida's golden droplet, lost on a Marseille street.

Sixteen

THE FILM CREW were rushing around in the Rue Richomme, being ordered about by a corpulent personage whom everyone called Monsieur Mage. They had spotted a sewer grate by the side of the pavement and the cameraman had trained his viewfinder on it, at the same time making sure that he had the latitude for a panoramic shot. But the main attraction for the onlookers was a clown—a circus Auguste with a red pasteboard nose and enormous shoes—who was to be the only actor in the sequence they were now shooting. In the midst of these gray, pale people he stood out like a grapefruit in a pile of potatoes. Monsieur Mage was now standing still, and, with an earnest air that accentuated his natural squint, he was looking at Idris, who, leaning on his brush, was himself observing the clown. Monsieur Mage beckoned to the gray-haired man with him.

"You see that little street sweeper? Sign him on."

"Sign him on? To do what?"

"His job, for goodness' sake! Get him to sweep. In the gutter."

The gray-haired man went up to Idris. He took a two-hundred-franc note out of his wallet and gave it to him.

"Sweep! Come on, get sweeping! You can forget everything else. For rehearsal, please. Everyone in position."

Idris, resigned to not understanding, began to trail his brush along the gutter. The clown came up with an uncertain, hesitant gait, looking for something. He noticed a fence, ran and looked over the top of it, abandoned that tack and went and examined the gutter and Idris's brush. Then he stopped short in front of the sewer grate. With his tentative gait, he described a semicircle around the grate. Then he went up to it and knelt down on the asphalt. His face expressed despair, hope, expectation. Crouching down by the sewer grate, he plunged first his hand into it and then his whole arm. You could feel the effort he was making to try to reach something that was no doubt very far down in the stinking darkness of the sewer. At last his face lit up. A broad smile spread over it. Slowly, the clown stood up, holding a beautiful red rose in his hand. With his legs twisted around each other, his free hand gently caressing the air, his eyes voluptuously closed, he was now breathing in the perfume of the rose.

"Great!" shouted Monsieur Mage. "We'll go for a take. Everyone in position. Hey, you there, the sweeper—back where you started from. And get sweeping, for God's sake!"

"YOU MEAN to say they got you to act in a film?"

Achour couldn't get over it.

"They even gave me two hundred francs!" Idris said in confirmation, pulling out his wallet.

"He's only just left Tabelbala and he's already a film star! What a guy! You've certainly got what it takes. And I thought *I* was smart!"

"What's more," Idris added, "the director noticed me. He gave me his card and told me to phone him."

Idris handed him a visiting card the color of Parma violets, on which Achour read:

ACHILLE MAGE
Filmmaker
13 Rue de Chartres   Paris XVIII

He held it up to his nose.

"Judging by the color and the smell, he must be quite someone! And then, it's not far from here. Are you going to phone soon?"

"Who, me?"

Idris suddenly felt out of his depth. To use a telephone, especially to call an unknown and apparently important man— that was really asking too much of him.

"Maybe. Later on. We'll see."

"Mustn't let things like that pass you by."

"There'll be others."

"What a guy! I don't know whether I ought to laugh or cry. In one sense, though, maybe you have *baraka* because you've only just arrived. You don't know the first thing about anything, and it shows in your face. And above all, you still carry your desert and your oasis with you. You don't even realize it. But even though I've already been swallowed whole by Paris, I can feel there's something about you that attracts people's attention. It's like a charm. It won't last. Make the most of it."

"I already lost a lot in Marseille. The evening I arrived. With a whore."

Achour guffawed.

"That, my cousin, isn't serious! In one sense, though, since it had to happen, it's just as well that it already has. All the same, I hope you haven't caught anything."

"Caught, no. Lost, I tell you. Lost."

Achour looked at him, not understanding. But Idris didn't add a word of explanation.

Seventeen

THE MENU—illuminated, and all curlicued with arabesques —announced, in calligraphic lettering:

Au Képi Blanc
Specialties: Méchoui, Tagine, Couscous
Moorish Decor

The façade of the establishment looked like a combination of an army blockhouse, a North African shrine, and the palace in *The Arabian Nights*. A waiter wearing a chechia and baggy trousers was stationed at the door. Idris went up to the menu and became absorbed in reading it. The words danced in front of his eyes without conjuring up anything precise in his mind: bisteeyah of pigeon with cinnamon, seksu in milk, brikks with honey, chakchoucka with eggs, chorba with herbs, bourek of onions, maktfah with vermicelli, dolma with pimentos . . .

"In your opinion, is couscous better with chicken or with lamb?"

Idris turned around. The young man who had addressed

him, his eyes deep-set in a bony face, was giving him a hard, ironic look.

"I don't know," Idris stammered. "I've never eaten couscous."

The young man went on staring at him.

"Well, what do you know! I'd have taken you for an Arab."

"No; I'm a Berber."

"Arab, Berber, it's all the same, isn't it?"

"No."

"Where do you come from, then?"

"From the Sahara. From an oasis in the northwest of the Sahara."

"You come from the Sahara and you've never eaten couscous?"

"No, never. In Tabelbala we're too poor to eat either chicken or lamb. We have a saying: the stomach is an empty bladder that experience has taught to shrink."

"What's your national dish, then?"

"I don't think we have a national dish. What we mostly eat is tazou, but you can't really call that a national dish."

"Tazou?"

"Semolina with carrots, cabbage, beans, eggplant, zucchini, chilies . . ."

"Enough to take the roof off your mouth, eh! What about meat?"

"No. Maybe a bit of a camel bone . . ."

A few minutes later they were squatting at one of the low tables in the restaurant in front of a sumptuous fish couscous. The luxurious, darkened lighting was conducive to the dreams and memories of Idris's new friend.

"I took one look at you and I told myself: it's the Sahara come to meet me!"

"The Sahara," said Idris. "I learned that in France. We don't have a word for it."

"The Sahara—the desert, you know!"

"We don't have a word for desert."

"All right; words, I agree, are my business. I'll explain the Sahara to you."

"The French always have to explain everything. But I never understand a thing about their explanations. One day a blond Frenchwoman came to where I live. She photographed me. She told me, 'I'll send you your photo.' But I never received anything. So now I've come to work in Paris. Photos—I see them everywhere. Photos of Africa too, of the Sahara, the desert, the oases. I don't recognize anything. They tell me, 'That's your country; that's you.' Me? That? I don't recognize anything!"

"It's because you don't know. You must learn. After all, French children learn about France at school. I shall teach you what Idris-from-the-Sahara is."

"And why don't you teach me something about yourself too?"

"That's true, what am I thinking of! Who am I? I am the Marquis Sigisbert de Beaufond, at your service!"

And he half stood up, and bowed to Idris.

"One of the oldest families from the soil of the Franche-Comté. Yes, monsieur. And I may add that a fat lot of good that does me! I was a rebel, a dropout, unteachable. Expelled from the kindergarten in Passy, from the Christian Brothers' school in Neuilly, by the Oratorians in Pontoise, by the Jesuits in Évreux, by the Lazarists in Sélestat, by the Ignorantines in Alençon. I ran away from home for the third time when I was seventeen and found myself in Sidi-bel-Abbès, where I joined the Foreign Legion with forged papers. Ah, Idris, the Legion! The epic of the white kepis. Actually, the owner of this restaurant is an ex-Legionnaire. March or die! *Camerone!* The Duvivier film *La Bandera*, dedicated to General Franco, the head of the Spanish Legion. Gabin's first great role. The clash with Pierre Renoir: 'I'm giving you a week in jail for intending to kill me, and another week for not having done so when you had the chance!' And Pierre Benoit, *L'Atlantide!* Brigitte Helm as Antinéa. "What a devastating day! What a heavy, heavy night . . . One is no longer oneself, one no longer knows . . .'

" 'Yes,' says the far-off voice of Saint-Avit. 'A heavy, heavy night, as heavy, you know, as the night I killed Captain Morhange.' And behind all that, the mystical vision of Charles de Foucauld, the saint of the Assekrem: "Think that you are to die a martyr, stripped of everything, lying on the ground, unrecognizable, covered with blood and wounds, violently and painfully killed, and hope for it to be today.'

"But you know, Idris, of all the episodes in the Saharan epic, the one I lived through the most intensely was the death of General Laperrine in March 1920, during his attempt to create an air link between Algiers and Niger. The strangest thing was that this former commander of the oasis region, this companion of Charles de Foucauld, this creator of Saharan companies, well, it was by pure chance that he embarked on this mortal adventure! I met the pilot of his plane, Colonel Alexandre Bernard, on the farm in the Bresse where he ended his days. He gave me an account of the tragedy. Listen carefully, Idris: it's a real epic!

"What they were trying to do, then, was to establish the first air link between white Africa and black Africa. Two flights of three planes were to take part, one leaving from France and the other from Algiers. Of the three planes leaving from France, one crashed at Istres, the other turned a somersault at Perpignan, and only the third made it to Algiers. So there were four aircraft that took off from Algiers on February 16. The one piloted by Alexandre Bernard was supposed to take General Nivelle, who was in command of the 19th Corps in Algiers. But their troubles weren't over. Nivelle was urgently recalled to Paris, so he had to withdraw. The plane was badly tuned and had to return to Algiers after only an hour in the air. Because in those days planes were made of wood and canvas with wing bracing. At night, the variations in temperature warped the struts and before they took off they had to reset and balance them, in much the same way as a violin is tuned before a concert.

"The first stage of the journey took them to Biskra, where General Laperrine lived. Seeing that Nivelle had had to give up the trip, he quickly decided to take his place in Bernard's plane. And anyway, it's something of an exaggeration to talk about his place. In actual fact there were just a couple of holes in the fuselage, one for the pilot and the other for the flight engineer, who on this occasion was Marcel Vasselin, a lad of twenty. So Laperrine had to sit on Vasselin's lap, which meant that he was abnormally exposed to the buffeting of the wind. The plane flew at 130 kilometers an hour, with a cruising range of five hours. The instrument panel consisted of a rev counter, an altimeter, a clock, and a water gauge. No compass, no radio, no mike to communicate with the other members of the team. Now and then Laperrine would scribble a note and have it passed to the pilot.

"Their next stopping place was In Salah. No plane had ever landed at that oasis. The event was celebrated with great jubilation. Then the aircraft that had come from Paris started on the flight back to Algiers. Only two planes were to carry on toward the south, the one with General Joseph Vuillemin on board, the other, piloted by Bernard, with Laperrine and the flight engineer, Vasselin. Naturally there was no question of covering the 690 kilometers between In Salah and Tamanrasset in one flight. They landed at Arak, in the middle of jagged gorges, and arrived the next day, February 18, at Tam. These first 2,300 kilometers, covered in record time and in ideal weather conditions, had made us confident. Dangerously confident. Our euphoria knew no bounds. The long-distance flight from Algiers to Niger was taking its course with almost disappointing ease. South of Tam, however, we were plunging into the unknown. True, we had sent messages to the natives asking them to mark out our route with drawings on the ground and big brushwood fires. But after hours of flight we found ourselves in a fog of dense sand. Our plane was faster than Vuillemin's, but it only had enough fuel for five hours, compared to Vuillemin's ten. The two teams lost sight of each other. Laperrine ordered me to climb above the clouds to more than 3,000 meters, to try to regain contact. In vain. He passed me message after message. 'I'm sure the wind is making us drift eastward,' he wrote. Personally, I had another worry. My tank was practically empty. We had to land. It was midday when I went into a glide, and that increased our drift. I'd have done better to go into a spiral dive. The ground didn't look too bad. At first the plane taxied normally. But as it slowed down the wheels pressed down more heavily on the sand, and suddenly the hard surface collapsed. The wheels stuck. The plane did a nosedive and turned a somersault. Laperrine, still perched on Vasselin's lap, was thrown out onto the ground. We didn't at first suspect that he was badly hurt. We extricated ourselves from the great canvas bird lying on its back with its feet in the air. Laperrine was complaining of his left shoulder. I rubbed it with a lotion that was very popular at the time, Arquebuse. He fainted. We discovered later that he had fractured his collar-bone and broken several ribs. When he regained consciousness he assumed full control of the operations. He decided that we would go on a reconnaissance march toward the west, and then return to the plane, which had the advantage of signaling our presence. So we walked for several hours along crumbly ground that caved in with every step we took. When we stopped, exhausted, there was still nothing to be seen. Just on the off chance, we fired three shots close together, the conventional distress signal. After that we turned around and retraced our footsteps. If the wind had obliterated them, it's unlikely that we would have found the plane again. And it contained our water supply. We discovered, in fact, that its radiator contained eighteen liters of water, a providential supplement to what we had in our cans. The radiator was upside down, with its opening underneath it, but luckily not a single drop had leaked out. Laperrine decided that we would each drink a cupful of water every three hours. We were to use his silver drinking goblet, a present from the Duke of Aumale, who defeated Abd-el-Kader in 1843. Wherever he went, he took it with him. What do you think of that, my boy? Laperrine getting us to drink out of the Duke of Aumale's silver goblet every three hours?

"And our wait began, every day absolutely like the previous one, with glacial nights and middays like a furnace. At the beginning we ate a little, but as we became progressively dehydrated, after the eighth day we couldn't swallow a thing. On the fifteenth day, Laperrine's mouth was covered with blood. The next day he became delirious. The following morning, he didn't even stir. I noticed that ants were running over his open eyes. He was dead. We buried him in the furrow dug out by the plane. We covered the pit with a piece of canvas. We had the bizarre idea of putting the spare wheel on the canvas and the general's kepi on top of it. We didn't yet know that his death was going to save us! We took the heroic decision to decrease our water ration by half: a third of a liter every twenty-four hours, when we would have needed six to seven liters to make up for our dehydration. On the twenty-third day we hadn't a single drop of water left. We drank the famous Arquebuse lotion, all the bottles in our first-aid kit—iodine, camphor oil, paregoric elixir. We ate our toothpaste. Finally we decided to kill ourselves. How? By drinking, for God's sake, by drinking! By drinking what? Our own blood. There was a razor. We made deep slashes in our wrists. But that was a disappointment: not a drop of blood flowed. Just white wounds. We were too dehydrated. Here—look."

He held out his wrists to Idris.

"You see these white lines on my skin? They're the scars."

"No," Idris admitted honestly. "I can't see anything."

"The light isn't good enough in here," Sigisbert explained.

Then, after a moment's silence, he took up the thread of his dream again.

"These white wounds, well, they finally decided to bleed, but only after three whole days of watering. Because we were saved! One day—it was March 25—Vasselin told me he'd heard a camel roar. I answered that he was delirious. But soon I too heard sounds of life in the mineral silence of the desert. I jumped for my rifle and fired three shots into the air. It was a rescue party, the one under the command of Lieutenant Pruvost. Only, when they heard my shots, instead of speeding up they halted. They made their camels kneel, and then we saw a line of sharpshooters in battle formation advancing on us. It was ridiculous, but we were saved.

"And now I'm going to tell you two more things that are barely believable. Someone threw me a gourd. And I drank. I drank just as much as the Duke of Aumale's silver goblet would hold. Not a drop more! That had become my eighthourly ration. I wasn't thirsty for a single drop more. We had to reaccustom ourselves to being thirsty and to quenching our thirst.

"And this too, which is much more serious. You probably think, don't you, that the advent of the rescue party filled Vasselin and me with intense joy? Don't you believe it. The truth is that they had come too late. Too late, yes; we were already quite a way down the path to death. We were already more dead than alive. These men who were a hundred percent alive, with their jangle of camels and supplies, well, they disturbed us. We'd paid dearly enough, hadn't we, for the right to die in peace?

"And in any case, we soon became aware of the hell this unexpected rescue had plunged us into. We were incapable not only of walking but also of staying on a camel. So they improvised a couple of stretchers for us and lashed them to a camel's flank, and in this sorry state they took us to Tamanrasset. Oh, not in one go! We had to make halts of several days, sometimes, when we were so exhausted that it looked as if we might die in those infernal litters.

"You see, Idris, what impresses me most in this whole story is the work we had accomplished, through unspeakable suffering, to pry ourselves loose from life. Whereupon, up come these devils in the camel corps, just in time to grab us by the feet and pull us back into their realm, to drag us back into life again, into all the misery of life . . ."

Eighteen

ONCE AGAIN the little steel ball began to roll down the super-bonus runway, setting off an avalanche of luminous and sonorous signals around the female cowboy on the big display board. Channeled by the pins, it very gently came to rest in one of the 5,000-point cups. It shot up again, hit the glass, bounced off the central bumper up to the top of the slope, and then began to race down the length of the table toward the exit hole. This was where Big Zob's incomparable virtuosity manifested itself. A very light tap with the palm of his hand on the side of the table deflected the ball just in time and it landed on one of the flippers. Zob allowed it to glide two-thirds of the way down toward the plunger, and then . . . shoot! The ball, sent careering back sky high, once again began to roll down the super-bonus runway. Two sharp clicks announced the free games added to the others on the scoreboard. The adolescents crowding around the table looked up at Big Zob's smallpox-pitted face. This was the mute, fervent tribute of his fans, dazzled by his marvelous mastery. One of them murmured, "Just look at that—it's out of this world!" There was no sign that

Zob was affected by this adulation. His heavy lids remained lowered over his bulging eyes. No smile raised the bitter downward curve of his mouth. He was now playing with only one hand, allowing it to be clearly understood that he had lost interest. Then he wrenched himself away from the table, royally abandoning the five free games he had just won to the adolescents jostling to take his place.

Idris, riveted to the spot in admiration, watched him shuffling off. The Electronic was ablaze with all its multicolored neon lights at the corner of the Rue Guy-Patin and the Boulevard de la Chapelle. According to the time of day, its best customers were either people who had just come out of the Barbès overhead métro station or the staff of the Lariboisière hospital. But Idris was attracted by the games room, where whole batteries of Scopitones, pinball machines, and jukeboxes were being made to crackle and flash by young men whose helmets, boots, and trousers made them all seem identical. He dreamed of becoming accepted by these boys his own age.

"Here—I'll stand you a game of baby-foot."

Idris looked around. If the invitation had come from one of the adolescents, he would have been overjoyed. But it was a corpulent old man, dressed in light gray flannel, with a pink open-necked shirt and a mauve scarf. He was observing Idris through thick-rimmed spectacles, his gaze distorted by a slight squint.

"But it's my little street sweeper!"

The man shook Idris's shoulder affectionately. He was Achille Mage, the director who had given him two hundred francs for his work as an extra. He had even given him his card, and Achour had reproached his cousin for not yet having telephoned him. "It won't be long before he forgets you!"

Mage had apparently not forgotten Idris, and he didn't seem to hold it against him that he hadn't phoned. He looked at his watch.

"Rather than stay here, let's go and have a drink at my place," he suddenly decided.

As he led him out, Idris protested:

"But I don't drink alcohol."

"I have something else to offer you. It's called Palm Grove. Do you know those young lads in the Electronic?"

"No, they never talk to me," Idris admitted.

"*I* know them. All of them. And they know me. Even though they never talk to me in public. And they all noticed that we left together. Even Big Zob, who was hanging around on the pavement. Keep on not talking to them. And the less you go to the Electronic, the better it will be."

"But that was where you found me."

"Well, you had to go there to meet me! But now you have, that's it. Right?"

They had crossed the Boulevard de la Chapelle and passed under the overhead métro. By way of the Rue Caplat, they came to the medina of Paris, exclusively populated by Africans. Suddenly Mage stopped and pointed to the blue nameplate at the Rue de Chartres.

"Chartres! Do you realize the enormity, 'l'hénaurmité,' as Flaubert said?

A Beauceron am I. Chartres is my cathedral!

Poor Péguy! If he could see that! In the absence of a cathedral, this is where I have my little love nest. At number thirteen, my lucky number, because with me, you know, everything is always the wrong way around."

He stopped outside a sordid-looking building with a blackened porch opening onto the street.

"Note the layout of the place. The courtyard is open to all comers. You pass under the porch, and there you are. You can even ride straight into the courtyard on a moped, if you see what I mean."

"No."

"The electronicians you were with just now all have their firecrackers. When I hear someone revving up in my courtyard, I know I have a visitor. Because I have three windows overlooking the courtyard. But there's no point in trying to see which one it is who's in need of a little pocket money. They all look alike in their helmets. So I have to wait, my heart beating with impatience, to find out who is climbing my three floors and ringing my doorbell. It's the chef's surprise. The most fascinating thing of all is that my predictions are always wrong. But in the end, they all come. They know that the house specialty is worth the journey. All except one: Big Zob. Obviously, with his ugly mug and his carcass, he hasn't got much to sell. And yet Big Zob is never short of anything. It took me some time to tumble to it. What finally enlightened me was the fact that everything happened rather too well. I mean: never a whole lot of them jostling in the courtyard or on the stairs. Never too long without any of them either. A harmonious succession of pyrotechnical visits, as varied as they are regular. Odd, isn't it? And then I did what Voltaire did, when he looked up at the sky and said that the universe baffled him, because it was so like a clock, and he couldn't imagine such a clock existing without a clockmaker. I looked for the clockmaker, who, naturally enough, gets paid by his clock, I mean by the young electronicians, whose circulation he regulates."

He stopped on the third-floor landing, felt for his keys, and said to Idris:

"And, do you know why I'm telling you all this?"

"No."

"It's not, believe me, for the cynical pleasure of exposing the turpitudes of my private life. It's to stop you from hanging around at the Electronic, where the frightful Zob would like nothing better than to incorporate you into his flock, by fair means or foul. Do you understand?"

"Not everything, I think."

They were now in a little flat whose comfort was in striking contrast to the squalor of the building.

"You see," Mage commented, "outside, everything is filth and stench, muck and degradation. You push my door open:

here, everything is luxury and beauty, calm and voluptuousness. You really don't understand, then? Sit down there. Opposite me. But tell me, young fellow, where have you come from that you're so naïve?"

"I'm living in the Sonacotra hostel in the Rue Myrha."

"No, before, I mean. Algiers? Bône? Oran?"

"Tabelbala."

"Ta what?"

"Talbelbala. An oasis in the middle of the desert."

Mage stood up abruptly. He went up to Idris and stared at him, which accentuated his squint.

"In the middle of the desert . . . in the sand?"

"Sand—there's no shortage of that, but it's mainly stones. The reg, it's called."

Mage straightened up, seeming at a loss. He almost tottered over to the desk and came back with a sheet of drawing paper and a yellow felt pen.

"If you will be so good—draw me a camel."

"What? A camel?"

"Yes. Draw me a camel."

Obediently, Idris set to work. Mage went over to his bookshelves. He took out an illustrated album, went and sat down opposite Idris again, and changed his glasses. Then he read aloud:

And so I lived alone, without anyone I could really talk to, until my plane came down in the Sahara desert six years ago. Something in my engine had broken. And as I had neither mechanic nor passengers with me, I had to try to make a difficult repair on my own. It was a question of life and death for me. I had barely enough drinking water for a week. The first night, then, I slept on the sand a thousand miles from any human habitation. I was far more isolated than a shipwrecked sailor on a raft in the middle of the Ocean. Imagine my surprise, then, at daybreak, when a strange little voice woke me. It said:

"I know a lot about goats, sheep, and camels," Idris said, giving him his drawing. "That's all I saw, all through my childhood."

"And that was how," Mage went on, raising his eyes to him, "that was how in the middle of my solitude, with my engine broken, I saw the Little Prince of the sands arrive—you, Idris."

Idris stood up, to try to shake off the phantasmagoria once again threatening to imprison him in a kind of net of images.

"Another story I don't understand. Ever since I left it, everyone's been talking to me about the desert. In Beni-Abbès, they've put it in a museum. In Béchar, they've painted a picture of it. In Marseille, I saw a poster about the paradise of the oases. I had dinner with a marquis. He told me about Monsieur Benoit's Antinéa, and General Laperrine, Father de Foucauld and the Foreign Legion. And now you with your little prince. I don't understand any of it, and yet the desert is certainly where I was born."

"Yes, but solitude, my solitude. What do you make of solitude?"

"Solitude—what's *that?*"

"I've already told you, it's a broken-down engine and nobody, d'you hear me, nobody! And then all of a sudden you arrive with your pretty little wog's mug, just the sort I like!"

He had taken him by the shoulders. He squeezed his cheeks in his hand and shook him affectionately.

"Now listen to me, Idris of my heart, Idris of my ass. *You* are a poor down-and-out, because you turn up with your curly hair and your swarthy complexion. *I* am rich and powerful. I make films for television, that's my profession. I know all Paris. I call Yves Montand *tu,* and Jean Le Poulain and Mireille Mathieu. I lunch with Marcel Bluwal and Bernard Pivot. But the real truth is that I too am a poor down-and-out, and I need you. I need you, d'you hear me? It's unhoped for, isn't it?"

"You need me—what for?"

"What for, what for! Are you putting on an act or are you really feebleminded? To live, for God's sake!"

He turned, and took a few steps in the room. Then he came back and sat down, and went on in a calmer voice:

"As of tomorrow, I'm starting work on a publicity film in the Francoeur studios. I'm taking you on. You've already worked for me anyway. I need you for my film, you see."

Idris went and sat down facing him. Once again absorbed in professional matters, Mage explained:

"It's a commercial for a fruit soda, Palm Grove. Yes, the muck's called Palm Grove. I must have some samples in my fridge. Next summer, thanks to me, the whole of France will be drinking Palm Grove. It begins in the desert, then. Two explorers, half dead with thirst, are dragging themselves through the sand with a camel. Suddenly, they're saved!"

"HOW MUCH did Biglou give you?"

Idris had gone down into the Rue de Chartres alone. He had a date for the next day with Mage and his crew at the Francoeur studios. But he didn't get far. The three booted and helmeted young men must have been lying in wait for him. They wedged him up against a door. The one who interrogated him was Big Zob. Idris recognized him immediately, in spite of his helmet.

"We saw you going up with Biglou. How much did he give you?"

"Biglou?"

"Yes. Or Monsieur Mage, if you prefer. That's what he's called in the Electronic. Don't act dumb. Hand over the cash!"

"He didn't give me anything, I swear!"

"Search him!"

Idris made a vague gesture of defense against the hands of the other two, who were beginning to explore his pockets. A slap sent his head back against the door. But the search produced only a few coins. Zob looked at them contemptuously, and then threw them down onto the pavement.

"Get this into your head, you poor dope. Biglou belongs to us. There's no way you're going to be allowed to exploit him for yourself. You get the maximum out of him, okay? After which you come to the Electronic and hand over all of it. All of it, is that clear? To me or to one of these two here. A second slap emphasized these peremptory instructions. The trio withdrew on their high-heeled boots. Idris straightened up, rubbed his face, and began to look for his money between the paving stones and in the gutter.

ACHOUR LISTENED, shaking his head sadly.

"They beat you up, then?"

"A bit; not too much," Idris specified.

"And Monsieur Mage, what else did he say to you?"

"He also said, 'The boys call me Biglou because there's something coy about the way I look. But to say I squint would be pure calumny.' "

"You've got a good memory. And he gave you a drink?"

"Yes, his new drink. Palm Grove, it's called. It's quite nice. There's no alcohol in it. It's Palm Grove he's going to make a film about with me. A thirty-second film that'll also have the singer Mario in it."

"Does he smoke?"

"No. He offered me a cigarette. I said I didn't smoke. He said, 'Neither do I. It's twenty years since I smoked my last cigarette. These days the only taste of tobacco I get is on boys' lips. It's become the odor of desire, for me.' What does that mean?"

"You've got a terrific memory. You learned all he said by heart. But really, you don't understand very much."

"It's because I don't understand half of what he says that I remember it by heart. That makes up for it a bit."

"What else did Monsieur Mage say?"

"He said, 'What I see in boys' eyes is the image of a fat, sentimental, squint-eyed queen, lousy with money. I can't get myself to believe that that's me.'"

"Has he really got a lot of money?"

"He says he has. So do the boys. It must be true. About money, he said, 'Money goes marvelously well with sex. Giving money to a boy is making yourself his owner, it's already making love with him. In some cases that can even be enough. The money he steals from me belongs to him. Sex goes beyond the bounds of ownership.' What does all that mean?"

"What else did he say to you?"

"He said that we have a date and that I must be sure to keep it. I wrote it down: 27 Rue Francoeur, tomorrow morning at ten."

"He must have been thinking of a different sort of date, but that's too complicated for you."

"It isn't my fault, I come from somewhere else."

Achour remained silent for a moment, trying to follow an idea which, though luminous, was difficult to pin down.

"There's one thing that strikes me, you know. Yes, okay, you come from somewhere else. You come from Tabelbala. So do I. It's a funny thing, though, no one's ever photographed *me*, and when I arrived here, people tended to leave me in peace. With you, it starts with the blonde in the Land-Rover who takes your picture. After that, it never stops. Have you been to the cinema yet?"

"No," Idris admitted. "I keep meaning to, but something always stops me."

"That really is extraordinary! Because the rest of us, who have nothing, we only have dreams to keep us going, and dreams, well, we get them from the cinema. The cinema turns you into a rich, civilized man who goes around in beautiful convertibles, who lives in luxurious bathrooms, who kisses perfumed women, loaded with jewels, on the mouth. The cinema is our schoolteacher. When you come from the backwoods, how to walk on a pavement, how to sit down in a restaurant, how to take a woman in your arms—it's the cinema that teaches you all that. How many of our people are there who only make love in the cinema! You've no idea. It's even very dangerous for our girls, because the cinema teaches them things that they take home with them afterward. And their father or their older brother gives them a going-over with his fist or a stick, to get them to forget the filthy habits they've picked up at the cinema. And you, here you are, and you don't go to the cinema, but you act in it! You get photographed, you get filmed, and tomorrow it's going to start all over again!''

"It isn't my fault," Idris repeated.

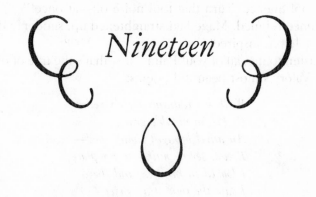

Nineteen

EVERYTHING WAS GOING WRONG on the No. 5 set in the Francoeur studios. Mario's black mane and Jovian beard no longer radiated royal optimism. Sweat glistened on his made-up torso. His paunch drooped mournfully over his paper palm-leaf skirt. Mage stood in front of him, grimacing. They had reached the critical moment in the shooting when the desperate director can see only one solution: to assume the roles of all the actors himself, having already taken over the functions of the cameraman, the gaffer, and the sound man. It was in this charged atmosphere that Achille Mage most fully revealed his genius. With the inspiration born of panic, he became visibly metamorphosed into a variety singer. He became Mario, the real Mario, the one they had engaged, bursting with communicative vitality.

"Palm, Palm, Palm, Palm Grove," Mage sang, performing contortions under the hypnotized eye of the singer. "Look, I'm strong, I'm lively, I'm aglow. And why? I ask you. Because I drink Palm, Palm, Palm Grove . . . Music, please!"

The amplifier obediently relayed the Palm Grove signature

tune. Mage, in a frenzy, began to dance, squinting alarmingly through his spectacles. Then he came to an abrupt halt.

"Stop! Silence! Turn that foul noise off—at once!"

Silence reigned. Mage had straightened up, suddenly dignified, solemn, inspired.

"Listen to me, all of you! Palm . . . that's the title of one of Paul Valéry's most beautiful poems:

> *With his radiance barely veiled*
> *By his formidable grace,*
> *An angel brought simple food—*
> *Bread, serene milk—to my place.*
> *I looked in his eyes, and there*
> *I saw the sign of a prayer,*
> *And it said to my vision:*
> *"Be calm, be calm, remain calm!*
> *Feel all the weight of a palm*
> *Bearing its great profusion!"*

Saint Valéry, forgive us our ignominy! We'll go from the top, kids. Everyone in position. Board, please! Turn over."

The clapper ran in front of the camera with his board, shouting: "Palm Grove one, take fourteen!" In a papier-mâché Sahara, two "explorers" appeared, dressed in khaki and wearing tropical helmets, dragging themselves along, groaning. A skeletal camel followed them. One of the explorers collapsed. His companion propped him up. He groaned: "A drink! A drink!" The other asked him: "A drink? What do you want to drink?" The first explorer suddenly sat up, his face radiant, and pointed to the horizon: "Palm Grove!" "Palm Grove?" "But of course—a palm grove. We're saved!"

"Cut!" shouted Mage. "That's not it at all. You must realize that unless you put more conviction into it, it isn't funny. You've got to make people laugh—sure. But because of your conviction! That's the whole secret of a good commercial."

And in his turn, he mimed the two roles:

"A drink, a drink, what do you want to drink? Palm Grove!

Palm Grove? But of course—a palm grove, we're saved! Come on, we'll do it again. Everyone in position. Clapper, this is take fifteen. Come on, then, the camel. Where's the camel gone?"

He plunged behind the set in search of the camel. He finally found it in a corner of the studio with Idris, who was talking to it and stroking it.

"Ah, of course! *You* know how to talk to it. What are you talking to it in? Camel language?"

"No, in Berber. That's my language."

"Right, then tell it in Berber that we're going from the top. Come on, kiddos, everyone in position. Board!"

Once again the two explorers and the camel started their desperate trek through the desert. And then they came to a set covered with plastic flowers, where they were welcomed by a group of singers and girls, led by Mario. Everyone began to sing "Palm Grove" around a fountain disgorging a metallic-green liquid. Mage stopped them.

"Cut! It's still not right. Let's make it real, shall we? This isn't an operetta. If you don't believe in it, you won't sell it. That's the ABC of publicity. Publicity is honesty!"

And, indefatigably, he once again started to mime all the roles at the same time. When he was out of breath he stopped, and drank from a bottle someone handed him.

"Ugh! What's this muck? Palm Grove. I might have known it. Isn't there any beer? We'll go again. But to put a bit of heart into us, we'll all repeat the slogan: 'the Palm Grove palm.' All together now, even the crew: the Palm Grove palm! And now everyone must drink. One, two, three, go! And the camel? the camel's disappeared again. Idris, your camel! The camel's got to drink too. And even, hm, that would look more real, through a straw! Idris, bring in your camel and tell it in Berber that it's got to drink Palm Grove through a straw!"

LATE THAT NIGHT, all those who had taken part in the film were assembled in the Café Francoeur to celebrate the completion of the Palm Grove film. In spite of their fatigue, the atmosphere was euphoric. Actors and technicians surrounded Mage like irreverent but friendly courtiers.

"What *I* want to know is what's going on in the cutting room. Because all we do is get it in the can. We can only have a vague idea of what the timing demands. The slot only lasts something like forty-five seconds. Do you realize?"

"No, you can't possibly imagine that when you're shooting."

"The masterpieces of the cinema are created in the cutting room!" declared Mage, raising a finger.

"What's for sure is that the commercials are the cream of the cinema. From all points of view: technical, artistic, psychological."

"Yes, that's true. The only thing I watch on TV is the commercials. Compared with them, everything else is old hat."

"Me too. I've got a video, but only to record the commercials. Some evenings I treat myself to a whole wad of them before I go to bed."

Hearing these remarks, Mage was all jovial smiles.

"Aren't they sweet, my team! Are you saying that to flatter me? Because, you know who I am? I'm the Eisenstein of publicity!"

"The other day you said you were the Orson Welles of publicity."

"Why not? And tomorrow I shall say: the Abel Gance of publicity."

"He's incredible, this guy! He's the only one that counts. But what about us, eh, what are we? Don't we exist? Do you make your commercials all by yourself?"

"No no, no no," Mage conceded. "Cinematographic work, like the Gothic cathedral, is the work of a team, as Hegel wrote. Nevertheless . . . nevertheless . . . every team needs a brain!"

The boos that greeted this remark were interrupted by the arrival of a gray-haired little man, the property buyer, who still had some administrative matters to sort out. He bent over Mage.

"Listen, boss, it's about the camel. What do we do with the camel? It's tied up in the studio yard."

"The camel? What camel?"

For Mage, Palm Grove and everything pertaining to it already belonged to the dim and distant past.

"Well, the one in the commercial. The Palm Grove camel. What do we do with it?"

"What d'you mean, what do we do with it? We give it back to its owner, of course. We rented it for the duration, didn't we?"

"Far from it. The circus owner never agreed to rent us his camel. No no, he sold it to us outright. I did tell you. Only too glad to get rid of it. You can imagine—a decrepit old beast on its last legs."

"In that case," Mage exclaimed in a panic, "*we* own it?"

"Precisely," said the prop man mercilessly. It's your camel. What do we do with it?"

"In short," an assistant put in, "it's like the immigrant workers. We thought we'd rented them and would be able to send them home when we didn't need them anymore, and then we discover that we've bought them and that we've got to keep them in France."

Mage considered the matter, but, as was his wont, his thoughts went skidding off in an unexpected direction.

"Before anything else," he said, "I should like us to agree on a point of vocabulary. Are we talking about a camel or a dromedary?"

"It has only one hump," said the script girl. "So it's a camel."

"On the contrary, camels have two humps. This animal has only one, therefore it's a dromedary."

"No, it's a camel," the cameraman put in.

"A dromedary," Mage insisted. "Camel—*chameau. Cha* means 'two,' *meau* means 'hump.' *Chameau:* 'two humps.'"

"Not at all, it's the opposite. Dromedary—*dromadaire*. *Dro* means 'two,' *madaire* means 'hump.' Les îles Madères—the Madeira Islands—make two sort of humps on the surface of the sea. Hence *dromadaire:* 'two humps.' "

Mage banged on the table.

"Shut up, all of you! The only person here who knows what we're talking about is keeping dead quiet at the bottom of the table. Idris, my child, you are the cameleer or the dromedarian of our team. So go and get the animal and take it . . ."

Idris was already on his feet.

"Where shall I take it?"

"That's right—where d'you want him to take your camel?"

"Oh hell!" Mage groaned. "We've already done a day's work, haven't we? Bring me a telephone directory."

After a bit of coming and going, they found him a telephone directory. Having changed his glasses and licked his thumb, Mage began to leaf through it.

"ABC, Alphabetical Order, Abadie, Abat-jour, Abat-jour, Abat-jour . . . It's incredible how many lampshade factories there are in Paris! Paris, capital of the lampshade! It's all Paul Géraldy's fault:

> *Let us pull down the shade a little—*
> *When hearts speak, it's bright light they fear,*
> *And eyes can be seen much better*
> *When objects are not quite so clear . . .*

Ah, here's what I'm looking for: abattoir, abattoir. We've come a long way from Paul Géraldy, a very long way! Hm, there's one not so very far from here: Abattoirs Hippophagiques de Vaugirard, 106 Rue Brancion, XVth arrondissement. That'll do for the camel!"

Idris was already on his way.

"There's no great rush, stay with us a little longer, cameleer of my heart!"

IT WAS STILL DARK when Idris left the yard of the Francoeur studios, pulling the haughty, miserable shadow of the Palm Grove camel along on a rope. His memory had recorded the somewhat confused directions lavished on him as to how to get to the Vaugirard horse abattoirs. At all events, he had concluded that he had to cross the whole of Paris from north to south. The distance didn't alarm him, and he had all eternity in front of him. But a camel isn't a bicycle. The ridiculous, woebegone silhouette looming up in the gray, rainy Paris dawn amazed the passersby and irritated the policemen. Right from the start, one of them told him to get off the sidewalk and walk in the road, alongside the parked cars. But the double-parked delivery trucks constituted dangerous obstacles. One had a load of vegetables. Idris was alarmed to observe that the camel had plucked a cauliflower as it went by and was carrying its prize high up in the air, which might well have caused a riot among the market gardeners. He preferred to stop and let it eat its cauliflower in the gutter, which it did very slowly, with snorts of satisfaction. Then they set off again. The camel's soft pads kept slipping on the greasy road. The drizzle beaded its coat. And yet Idris felt strangely comforted by this gigantic, ungainly presence. He thought back to the Tabelbala regs, the Beni-Abbès sands. Circumventing the cars, stopping at traffic lights, going through underpasses, he heard Zett Zobeida's song singing in him:

> The dragonfly flutters low over the water
> The cricket creaks on the stone
> The dragonfly flutters and wordlessly twitters
> The cricket creaks and utters no word
> But the dragonfly's wing is a skit
> But the cricket's wing is a script
> And this skit thwarts the tricks of death
> And this script tells the secret of life.

They came to a high wall, behind which there seemed to be some trees. After this night of electric lights and cigarette smoke, Idris would have liked to rest in a garden. He found a vast, open gate. He went in. It wasn't really a garden, in spite of the greenery. It was the Montmartre cemetery. At this hour, it was deserted. Side by side with ostentatious chapels, some of the graves were simple rectangular slabs. Idris lay down on one of them and immediately fell asleep. How long did he sleep? A very short time, no doubt, but long enough to be transported to the other cemetery, in Oran, where Lala Ramirez had taken him. The old woman was there, roundly abusing him and shaking her fist with her skinny arm. She was abusing him in French and in a man's voice, and she finally shook him by the shoulders. A man with a mustache, wearing a cap with a shiny peak, was bending over Idris, ordering him roughly to get the hell out of there with his camel. Idris sat up on the tombstone. Only to see the camel devastating a nearby grave that had recently been embellished with flowers. Having finally found a wreath to its taste, it had begun to pull it to pieces, slowly and methodically. The man in the cap was choking with fury; he talked about despoiling of tombs and, being a professional, invoked Article 360 of the Penal Code. Idris had to get up, drag the camel away from its chrysanthemums, and try to find his way out of the labyrinth of monuments. They crossed a square, a market, a bus station. Idris had never before ventured so far out of the Barbès district. Never for a moment, though, did it occur to him to ditch the camel and go back to the hostel in the Rue Myrha. Somehow he felt responsible for the animal. It was compelling him to continue this ridiculous, sinister trek, but it represented a duty for the Saharan nomad he still remained. And anyway, as he began to leave the poorer districts behind and to enter the fashionable ones, it was clear that the passersby were more and more inclined to pretend not to see him. After the Gare Saint-Lazare, but even more so in the Place de la Madeleine and Rue Royale, nobody seemed to notice this strange couple among the hurrying, early-morning crowds. After a perilous crossing of the Place de la Concorde, he succumbed to the temptation to go down to the banks of the Seine to escape the inferno of the traffic. Patches of haze were drifting over the black water. Under the Pont Alexandre III, tramps, huddled together around a little fire built from street sweepings, called out to him merrily, brandishing empty wine bottles. A woman, hanging her wash out on a barge, stopped what she was doing and went and called a child to show it the camel. A dog came bounding up to it, barking. Once again, as the tissue of social relationships became less compact, the camel had become visible. Idris walked on past the riverboats, then went back up to the embankment, crossed the Pont de l'Alma in the direction of the Eiffel Tower, passed under its belly, his head raised, seeing nothing beyond its crisscross girders. The camel, so far totally indifferent to everything, suddenly shied, with a raucous snarl, at the sight of an old man holding a bunch of multicolored balloons on a stick. At last they found the Rue de Vaugirard, whose name rang in Idris's ears as the key to the labyrinth in which they had been forlornly wandering for several hours. He had in fact been told: Rue de Vaugirard, and then Rue Brancion, and in that street, at No. 106, the horse abattoir. He was making his way down the Rue des Morillons when he was surprised to see a herd of cows. The patter of their hooves on the macadam, their subdued lowing, and above all the smell of dung enveloping them were as surprising in these surroundings as was the presence of the Palm Grove camel. And anyway, it seemed that the camel was sensitive to the animal presence of the cows, for it quivered, gathered up its strength, and, passing Idris, broke into an awkward little trot and caught up with them. In this fashion they came to No. 40 Rue des Morillons, whose gate was surmounted by an ox's head made of golden metal. For indeed, if horses enter the place of death by way of the Rue Brancion, it's by way of the Rue des Morillons that bovines go to hell. A hell, moreover, that at first looks familiar and even reassuring. For Idris found himself in the middle of vast wooden stables full of straw, warm, giving out an agreeable smell of hay and dung, in a pleasant atmosphere of peaceful lowing, sighs, and sleepy movements. True, at the far end of the stalls there was a little door through which the cows were passing calmly, one after the other, without jostling each other, as if they were going to the milking parlor or out to graze. This door opened onto a gangway that led up to a vast room with a guillotine-type door. The cows waited on the gangway, each one's head resting on the rump of the one in front, full of confident resignation. They were like patient housewives, shopping basket in hand, waiting at a shop door.

The guillotine rises. The first cow moves forward. The guillotine falls behind her. She finds herself imprisoned in a cage a little above the ground. The killer waits until the plaintive head is placed in a suitable position. He brings his "matador" down in the middle of the forehead, between the big, apprehensive eyes gazing up at him. A sharp crack. The animal collapses onto its knees. The left-hand panel of the cage disappears and the huge body, shaken with spasms, topples over onto the grid covering the ground. The slaughterer bends down and cuts the carotid artery. Then he attaches the animal's right back hoof to a chain hanging from an overhead rail. The chain becomes taut and the carcass is raised by one hoof, like a rabbit brandished by a gigantic hunter. The carcass glides along the rail, while a vermilion fountain gushes down onto the grid. The left back leg thrashes the air convulsively. The warm, panting carcass joins its fellow carcasses crowded together in the slaughterhouse on enormous, funereal suspensions. Men enveloped from head to foot in white oilcloth attack them with choppers and electric saws. Stripped of their skin, immense lustrous surfaces appear, all gleaming muscles and mottled slime. Steaming mauve and green viscera cascade down into vats.

An employee was hosing away the organic waste and brown juices, which went cascading over to the drainage grids. Suddenly, he stopped in amazement. The tall silhouette of the camel had just appeared in the open doorway. He called a colleague.

"Good God! Come and have a look! What d'you think of that! Now we'll have seen it all, here: a Bedouin with his camel. Well, well, now we know that France has had it!"

Three or four knackers came up to Idris and his animal, guffawing.

"So you've brought us a camel, have you? You want us to turn it into steak? You've got a nerve, my lad!"

"Have *you* ever slaughtered a camel?"

"Who, me? What d'you take me for? And can you imagine any butcher wanting to buy that?"

The killer came down from his platform and said to Idris:

"Me know how kill cows and horses. Me no know how kill rhinoceroses. Where you hit it, to kill a camel? On its hump?"

"Here—I'll give you some good advice: take it back to Africa where it comes from. It ought never to have left its own country."

"Or take it to the lost and found office, it's just around the corner in the Rue des Morillons!"

IDRIS DECIDED TO LEAVE. But before he could get out, this shepherd had the misfortune to pass through the room where the sheep were slaughtered. There were about twenty of them, their throats cut, hanging by one foot, and they were swaying like so many censers, projecting their blood onto the walls and the people, a tragic, grotesque aerial ballet.

He didn't know where to go with his camel. All the fatigue of the night descended onto his shoulders. He turned into various streets at random, crossed avenues, crossed the Seine again. He had the vague intention of returning to the hostel in the Rue Myrha, but no idea of which way to go. He was attracted by some trees which were becoming increasingly numerous, a still-distant mass of foliage. It was a relief to be at last walking on the soft ground of a path running alongside the iron gates of sumptuous residences. The camel just managed to avoid a funny little blue-and-green train with its bell jingling madly. Children were crowding around a door with a ticket seller's window. It was the Zoo. Idris followed them and, thanks to the camel no doubt, he was allowed in without a ticket. He wandered about for a moment between the aviary containing the birds of prey and the "Enchanted River." Then he had a surprise: another camel had appeared, a she-camel to be precise, her little round ears flapping as a sign of welcome. The two animals rubbed flanks. Their morose, disdainful heads met very high up in the sky, and their big, pendulous lips touched. Under a thatched shelter Idris noticed saddled and bridled donkeys and a charming little varnished-wood cart, to which two goats were harnessed. Adolescents dressed as Turks —turbans, baggy silk trousers, and Turkish slippers—got to work on Idris's camel. They put an embroidered blanket over its back, a cloth with little bells over its ears, a muzzle over its mouth. Small children pushed and shoved each other up a kind of tall red ladder which was just the right height to enable them to perch on the camel's back.

Idris walked away, drunk with fatigue and happiness. He passed the Palace of Distorting Mirrors, and observed himself puffed up like a balloon, or on the contrary tall and skinny, or cut in half at the waist. He stuck out his tongue at these grotesque images of himself, the latest additions to so many others. A chorus of youthful laughs answered him. He saw his dressed-up camel passing majestically by, on its back a cluster of little girls shrieking with joy. The sun spread fans of light through the foliage. There was music in the air.

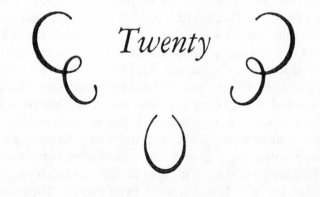

Twenty

IDRIS REMEMBERED the glass-fronted cabinets of the Saharan Museum in Beni-Abbès; they were shopwindows in miniature. But ever since he had been in Paris he had in fact done nothing but go from shopwindow to shopwindow. When he crossed a road, it was almost always because, once his eyes had had their fill of one window display, the goods in the shop opposite had beckoned to him. The small shops in the Barbès district overflow onto the pavement and offer to the hands of passersby piled-up racks of shoes, underclothes, and bottles of perfume. A shopwindow signifies a better class of establishment. But even then, it mustn't be confined to a single window which gives you immediate access to the shop, where you find its owner, his till, and the customers coming and going. No, a shopwindow worthy of the name is sealed off by a partition. It forms an enclosed area, at the same time totally exposed to the gaze and inaccessible to the hands, impenetrable and yet without secrets, a world you may touch only with your eyes but which is nevertheless real, in no way illusory like the world of photography or television. A fragile, provocative safe, a shopwindow is just asking to be broken into.

Idris had not finished with shopwindows. That evening, coming from the Boulevard Bonne-Nouvelle, he had turned into the Rue Saint-Denis, and he became aware of the call and smell of sex coming up from all sides. He remembered Marseille and the Rue Thubaneau. And yet the contrast between the two "hot" streets was immediately apparent. The girls here seemed younger; in any case, they were less corpulent, and none was of the African type. But it was above all with its flashing, multicolored shops, with the heavy curtains concealing their entrances, that the Rue Saint-Denis outclassed the Rue Thubaneau and gave itself an air of feverish, hidden luxury. "Sex Shop." "Live Show." "Peep Show." These words kept repeating themselves in flashing lights over the shop fronts. Their triple red grimace promised the young unmarried man, condemned to chastity by solitude and poverty, the satisfaction of his virile needs among showers of obscene images. He passed three small shops, and then pushed aside the curtain over the doorway of the fourth.

At first he thought he was in a bookshop. The walls were covered with books with garish covers and enigmatic titles: *My Wife Is a Lesbian; Mixed Doubles; X Nights; Three Vestas for One Cigar; Heads with Tails; Loves, Delights, and Orgasms; Woman Descends from Ape; The Hidden Face of the Moon*. With some difficulty, Idris deciphered these words which meant nothing to him. The photos on the covers, on the other hand, displayed a brutal, puerile eroticism that spoke more of abjection and burlesque than of beauty or seduction. Yet Idris could well see what reduced the violence of these images: the more completely the anatomical details of the genitals were revealed, the less the faces appeared. In many of the photographs they were even totally invisible. There was a kind of compensation in this. It seemed that by abandoning only the lower part of their bodies to the photograph, both men and women managed to deprive it of the essence of their real selves. Perhaps these butcher's displays were finally less compromising in their anonymity than the portraits, which were apparently more discreet?

The objects on the stands and shelves aroused few echoes in Idris's imagination. The "delicate lingerie" with the lace panties, garter belts, fishnet stockings, and bras conjured up no more than vague memories, but he remained totally perplexed by the collections of Japanese vibrators of all shapes and sizes and the simple, grooved, ringed, nodulous or barbed dildos, whose use escaped him. A panoply of S-M whips made of plaited cowhide and which writhed like snakes seemed to him by comparison more familiar and almost reassuring. A life-sized inflatable doll with buoyant curves and lacking in none of the charms of the feminine anatomy was standing stiffly, rounded and smiling, at the foot of a little staircase leading to the peep show. Idris went up it.

A man sitting behind a counter gave him change in five-franc coins, and pointed to the door of booth No. 6, whose red light was not on. It was a tiny room, almost entirely taken up by a huge leather armchair facing a concealed window. Idris sat down and looked around him. The floor, sticky with moist patches, was strewn with crumpled tissues. On the right-hand wall a metal box with a slot bore this laconic inscription: "2 × 5 francs = 300 seconds." Idris put the two required coins in the slot. Immediately an indicator lit up, showing the figure 300, which began to decrease second by second. At the same time the light in the booth went out and the screen over the window rose. The crack of a whip rang out against a background of languorous music. The scene was bathed in yellow light. The action took place on a slowly revolving turntable and was reproduced in a series of mirrors, the reverse side of the booth windows, which were made of oneway glass so that the spectators could not see one another. A woman-lioness was lying on her side across the revolving stage. She shook her splendid mane, with a bitter, twisted smile. Her midriff was squeezed into a golden fur garment that left her buttocks and bulging breasts exposed. She held her breasts in her hands and looked at them avidly with her slanting green eyes, then rubbed their nipples against her cheek and held them up in supplication toward one of the windows, as a mother might hold her children up to a hypothetical savior. Then she writhed on the floor, a prey either to pain or to voluptuousness —to voluptuous pain—still caressed, however, by the syrupy music, under the sightless gaze of the mirrors. At this point a new crack of the whip tore into the music. The lioness shuddered. Her big mouth, with its twisted smile, opened and emitted a silent roar. She arched her back and opened her thighs, revealing the yawning gap of her newly shaved vulva, which she began to claw at with the sharp-pointed red nails of one hand. Then she rolled over onto her stomach, and her buttocks rose and fell violently in time with the music.

The curtain fell over the window and the light in the booth came on again. Idris stood up, trembling with frustrated desire.

"YOU'RE CRAZY to want to meet her," Achour had told him. "It's as if that woman didn't exist."

"But she does exist," Idris had protested. "She was on the other side of the window. I could talk to her like I'm talking to you!"

"She existed for your eyes, but not for your hands. Here, everything's for our eyes, nothing's for our hands. Glass windows are like the movies and television—for the eyes, only for the eyes! You need to understand these things. And the sooner the better!"

But Idris still didn't understand these things, for the very next morning he went back to the Rue Saint-Denis. He had no difficulty in finding the sex shop again, but he didn't notice that the luminous sign advertising the peep show was not lit. He went into the shop. There was no one there to welcome him but the inflatable doll, still stiff, curvaceous and smiling, standing at the foot of the little staircase. He went up. The doors of all the booths were open. In one, he saw the back of a cleaning woman who was wielding a long-handled floor mop. She was dressed in a gray apron which revealed her naked legs, knotted with varicose veins. She stopped mopping and turned to empty a plastic rubbish bag full of crumpled tissues.

"And what might the young man want?"

Her pepper-and-salt hair was cut very short, her face was a mask hardened by the absence of makeup. She screwed up her eyes to try to get a better look at Idris, who stared at her in amazement. Those slightly slanting green eyes reminded him of something.

"If you've come for the peep, it doesn't start until five," she added.

And she went back into the booth to get her mop and bucket of water.

"These men! It's incredible how filthy they are! They squirt it all over the place. On the chair, on the walls, on the floor! Some even splash it over the window!"

And as she said these last words, her big mouth was distorted into the twisted smile of the whipped lioness.

Twenty-one

> Mamadou told me
> Mamadou told me
> We've squeezed the lemon
> Now we can ditch the skin.
> The lemons, they're all the niggers,
> Those black African children of sin.

THE IDOLS of the present generation are no longer called Idir the Berber, or Djamel Allam, or Meksa, or Ahmed Zahar, or Amar Elachat. These can still be heard, and even seen on tired old Scopitones. But they are no longer understood. The young of today recognize themselves in the rhythms and imprecations of Béranger and Renaud when they sing—in French —of the difficulty of living as an outsider, with one foot in unemployment and the other in delinquency.

> My moniker's Slimane and I'm fifteen,
> I live with my folks in a slum,
> Got my teacher's cert. in delinquency,
> I've had practice, I ain't no bum.

Got a snake tattooed up and down my arm,
In our gang, I'm number one.

Constantly force-fed with coins, the machine incited the young to hopeless rebellion against the conspiracies of the privileged classes. The customers from the Barbès métro milled around the bar and remained deaf to the vehement incantation fulminating behind them. Sitting alone at a table wedged up against the bar, Idris was lost in a book of comic strips. The atmosphere of the café vaguely merged into the adventures he was following, page after page. The words in the bubbles silently isolated themselves from the conversations, the calls, and the exclamations he could hear around him. Was he dreaming? The heroine of this story looked like the blonde in the Land-Rover, and also like the whore in Marseille. Furthermore, she was being driven in the Land-Rover by a man with a brutal face, in the Tabelbala reg. All of a sudden she asked him to stop and go back the way they came. She had seen something she wanted to photograph. Reluctantly, the man obeyed. The Land-Rover charged up to a herd of goats and sheep surrounding a young shepherd. It stopped. The woman jumped out. Her platinum-blond hair floated over her shoulders. She was showing her naked arms and legs. She was holding a camera.

"Hey, boy!" exclaimed the bubble coming out of her mouth. "Don't move too much, I'm going to photograph you."

"You might at least ask his opinion," muttered the man's bubble. "Some of these people don't like it."

"You're a fine one to say that!" remarked the woman's bubble.

Renaud's voice cut in abruptly:

We prowl the car parks ev'ry night
What we want's a flash car, not a heap,
We borrow it for an hour or two,
Then dump it out of sight.

We visit the hookers, but not to screw,
Just to think of as we go to sleep.

"Don't delude yourself," said the man's bubble derisively, "he's much more interested in the car than he is in you!"

The camera was drawn in close-up. It concealed most of the woman's face. A bubble came out of the box: "Click-clack." The photo had been taken.

"Give me the photo."

The bubble came from the shepherd, who was holding his hand out to the woman. She showed him a map she'd taken from the car. It too was in close-up, in the woman's hands. It was the north Sahara: Tabelbala, Beni-Abbès, Béchar, Oran.

"We'll send you your photo from Paris. Look. This is where we are, see? In Oran, we take the car ferry. Twenty-five hours on the sea. Marseille. Eight hundred kilometers on the autoroute. Paris. And there, we'll get your photo developed and printed."

I've put an ad in the local rag,
I'm looking for a nice young bird
Who'll get a job and keep me in grub,
'Cause for me, work's a dirty word!
It'd take a lot to make me sweat,
But I haven't found my dream girl yet . . .

The car drove off, raising a cloud of dust. But the comic strip followed it, and the conversation between the man and the woman escaped from it.

HE: "You see, you did disappoint him. And you must admit that you never had the slightest intention of sending him his photo."

SHE: "Well, at least *I've* never asked you for the photos you take of me."

HE: "No, *you* haven't. I don't take them for you. I have customers for them."

SHE: "Was it really necessary for us to go to the middle of

the Sahara for you to photograph me in the dunes and palm groves?"

HE: "Things have to be done properly. These things speak to the imagination of some men. Some Frenchmen like exotic decors. Some oil sheikhs like blond women. I photograph you in an oasis, and that keeps everyone happy."

SHE: "Everyone except the blond slave sold with the photo."

HE: "The blond slave thrives on her slavery, so long as it is gilded slavery. Between a comfortable cage and the poverty of freedom you chose the cage, and you've got nothing to complain about."

SHE: "Comfort isn't the only thing in life. And anyway, the suggestive photos you take of me, and circulate, compromise me more than all the rest. I have the feeling that I shall never be free of them. It's worse than if I were tattooed, because at least you can keep tattoos to yourself, and you can hide them. Whereas with these photos going the rounds here, there, and everywhere, if by any chance I were to meet a decent man who loved me, I'd always be afraid that one day they'd jump up and hit him in the face."

> *The colonists have gone, but they've taken in their traps*
> *Whole shiploads full of slaves, so's not to lose the knack.*
> *Menials to sweep their streets, that's what they've taken back.*
> *The slaves all look the same in their silly woolen caps,*
> *The chill pierces their bones, but it's their hearts it saps.*

Idris looked up. He was not in the least surprised to see the man and the woman of the comic strip leaning on the counter. He recognized them, even though they weren't dressed as they had been in the Land-Rover. It was perfectly natural for them to be there, and to continue their heated discussion.

HE: "In the meantime, I've found an enthusiastic amateur who's absolutely rolling in money. Your photos have, as you put it so well, jumped up and hit him in the face. I'm going to phone him to make a date. Waiter, a token please!"

SHE: "And what if I asked to see some photos of this customer who's rolling in money? Just for once, I'd like to know more or less where I'm going."

HE: "Have you gone crazy? You're not the one who pays, he is. So he's the one who chooses from photos. You can't reverse the roles, you know!"

SHE: "Whether you like it or not, one day I'm going to make my own choice. And I won't make it from photos. It'll be for real, from life."

HE: "That won't happen for a while. Because you'll have to reimburse me for my expenses first. I've made an investment, and I have no intention of letting myself be fleeced. And anyway, that's enough of that! I'm going to phone. Wait here."

Idris didn't know whether he was dreaming or living through a real scene. The Land-Rover blonde was alone, standing at the counter. She looked in his direction but didn't seem to see him. Either she was shortsighted or he had become transparent. The jukebox howled even more loudly:

> *If a cop's roughed up, if they croak a cop,*
> *Law and order's at risk—raise the alarm!*
> *State funeral for the valiant gendarme.*
> *Bring back the old values—this has got to stop!*
> *I bend over, and I puke—*
> *Can't wait till they all get nuked.*

Idris stood up and went over to the woman. He had taken the plunge—straight into the comic strip. He had all the audacity of an imaginary hero.

"Do you recognize me? I'm the boy you photographed in Tabelbala."

She didn't understand.

"What? What does he want?"

"It's me, Idris from Tabelbala. You told me: "I'll send you your photo." Look, it's written in the paper."

He showed her the comic strip.

"He's crazy. What's he talking about?"

[156]

She glanced briefly at the magazine, then looked around as if trying to get help.

"Come with me. He's a bad man. He wants to sell you. Come on!"

She shrank back against the bar, and knocked her glass over. Some of the customers stopped talking. Idris tried to grab her arm and take her away.

"Come on, we'll go together. The man's selling you with his photos."

The man in question had come back from the phone booth, and he flew to the aid of his protégée.

"What's this wog doing? Are you going to leave Madame alone? D'you want my fist in your face?"

Idris had time to recognize Big Zob coming up to intervene, surrounded with the halo of chivalrous zeal.

"Yes, you'd do well to take care of him. I've been watching him for quite a while. He's trying to abduct Madame."

Idris stood his ground.

"You're a bastard. You're selling the lady with your photos."

"Good God, d'you hear that? What does this moron think he's doing?"

He smashed his fist into Idris's face. The woman screamed, as a precaution. Zob stuck out a leg and tripped Idris, and he collapsed onto a table in the middle of the customers.

"WELL, THEN," said Achour, "so they took you to the police station?"

"Yes. I don't know how, but the cops were there right away. My nose was bleeding. Everyone was yelling at the same time. Especially the woman."

"In this district the cops are never very far away. But what got into you, for God's sake!"

"Then at the police station they asked me some questions, and a cop took it all down on a typewriter. My name, how

long I'd been in France, where I lived. They made me blow
into a little balloon. They made me dip my fingers into some
ink and put them on a card. And then they photographed me,
full-face and in profile."

"Yet again!"

"It isn't my fault; everyone photographs me."

"With your bloody nose and your black eye. A real murder-
er's mug, eh! And then what?"

"Then they phoned here to the hostel. They spoke to Isidore. Ten minutes later he was there, and he talked to the
cops, and they let me go with him."

"You can always rely on Isidore. But what got into you, for
God's sake!"

"It wasn't my fault, it was the comic strip, and there was the
music going full blast, and the blond woman. And anyway, I
wouldn't be surprised if it wasn't Big Zob—he probably set
the whole thing up on purpose."

They both fell silent, sitting on the bunk in their room,
looking at the floor, overwhelmed by fate.

Twenty-two

ACHOUR HAD TOLD HIM: "For that work, you'll need dungarees. You can get them at Tati's. Buy blue cotton ones, with a zip-up bib pocket." Idris had registered these details and gone to the Boulevard Rochechouart. He soon saw, though, that he had come to Tati Femme by mistake. Not knowing that a glassed-in footbridge over the Rue Belhomme led to Tati Homme, he once again went to the wrong place and, turning left on the pavement of the Boulevard Rochechouart, went into Tati Garçon. There was an atmosphere of youth and innocence about the displays of schoolboys' overalls, small check shirts and fancy track suits. Little boys in wax, their blue eyes twinkling with golden lashes, their arms outstretched in a gesture of self-conscious surprise, were pretending to be playing on crinkled-paper lawns strewn with footballs and tennis rackets. Two men, discussing one of these dummies, were standing in Idris's way.

"And when they're out of date or obsolete, what do you do with them? Chuck them on the rubbish heap?"

The man who had asked this question in a rather aggressive

tone had something of the young cock about him, with his crest of bristling hair, his pointed nose, and his eyes wide open in naïve indignation.

"We keep them in our storerooms until we get a chance to sell them to clothes shops in the provinces. I'm always being visited by small shopkeepers from Mamers, Issoire, or Castelnaudary who come here to buy little girls or boys, men or women. It even has a slave-market side to it, which is not without its piquancy."

The man spoke well, every so often stressing the irony of his remarks with a wry smile. Everything about him, and the casual tone he affected, suggested that he only condescended to the profession of display manager in a big store as an amusing pastime, quite unworthy to be taken seriously, and far inferior to his ambitions and capacities. He was observing the serious, passionate young man facing him as if he were a curious and totally ludicrous phenomenon, but all the more entertaining for that.

"But, if I may ask, what is it about these dummies that interests you?"

"I collect them," replied the young man with conviction. "Étienne Milan, photographer. I live just around the corner, in the Rue de la Goutte-d'Or."

"You collect shopwindow dummies?"

"Not indiscriminately."

"Children?"

"Boys. And boys from the sixties exclusively."

This time the display manager couldn't hide his stupefaction. He darted an anxious glance around him, as if to assure himself that his familiar surroundings had not disappeared without trace, and came face to face with Idris, who hadn't been able to help overhearing their conversation.

"Yes, but . . . why the sixties?"

"Because I was born in 1950."

"In short, these dummies of ten-year-old boys . . ."

"Yes. They're me."

[160]

The manager's eyes opened wide and his jaw seemed to fall. It's all very well to be of Sicilian origin, to be called Giovanni Bonami, to go in for commercial display, and to cultivate the style of the dandy-whom-nothing-can-faze; the arrival of such an oddball does nevertheless manage to throw you.

"Why don't we go and have a look in your storerooms?" Milan went on.

And, noticing Idris, who was still standing there in front of him:

"You might come with us, I shall need a bit of help," he said.

An elevator plunged them into the third basement. Under a very low ceiling whose fluorescent tubes shed a light that was both harsh and moonlike, there was the strangest sight: a vast, motionless ballet composed of hundreds of nude characters, petrified in gracious, sophisticated attitudes. The livid smoothness of their bodies even extended upward, and all these young, smiling, and made-up faces were rendered even more bizarre by their shiny, totally bald little heads.

"To me, they're incredibly erotic," Milan murmured.

"Are you aware," said Bonami, "that we are expressly forbidden by the police to dress or undress our dummies in the window within sight of anyone passing by? Our window dressers have orders to work behind a blind. Believe it or not, people have lodged complaints, claiming to be offended by this somewhat special form of striptease. It makes you wonder just how far prudery will go!"

"It isn't prudery," Milan retorted somewhat curtly, "it's the simple respect due to the dummies."

This contestation of the very essence of his personal domain, that of display, visibly irritated Bonami.

"I think you're wrongly confusing a dummy with a statue," he observed rather sharply. "Their relation to clothes is diametrically opposed. For the sculptor, the nude is of prime importance. In the ordinary way, a sculpture is nude. If it has to be clothed, the sculptor will first make it nude, and only later cover the body with clothes. The relation of the dummy to clothes is the reverse. Here, it's the clothes that are of prime importance. A dummy is only a by-product of clothing. It's as if it is secreted by its apparel. Hence its lack of charm when it is deprived of it. Whereas a statue, like the human body, may be naked. A dummy cannot be naked, it can only be dressed. What you see here are not bodies, nor even images of bodies. They are ectoplasms of suits, ghosts of dresses, specters of skirts, larvae of pajamas. Yes, larvae, that's probably the most appropriate word."

Milan seemed to be only mildly interested in the theories Bonami was propounding. He rapidly inspected the stiff, extravagant population surrounding him. Whereupon the display manager turned to Idris and began to ask him in a kindly way about his origins, his work, his place of residence.

"If you are available," he said, "I might have a job for you."

And, carried away by his deliberately nonchalant turn of thought, he couldn't help adding:

"It would even be an exciting, paradoxical experiment, more or less unique of its kind."

Idris looked at him with the most total lack of comprehension.

"This is what I am suggesting. The great majority of our clientele consists of Africans, and especially of Maghrebis. So it occurred to me that we might make some shopwindow dummies of the Maghrebi type, if you see what I mean. There's a workshop in Pantin where they make molds from living models—face and body. From one such mold they can make as many polyester dummies as they like. I think you might well be used as a model. It's quite well paid. Come and see me, if the idea appeals to you. But don't leave it too long, it will have to be very soon."

"What about those two—do you think I could have them?"

Milan was pointing to two bodies lying one on top of the other against the wall.

"Well! You certainly have a sense of charity! Those two

poor children were doomed to the scrap heap. And now they're saved!"

"I don't see any others that interest me."

Bonami had begun to disentangle the dummies and was carelessly pulling them by their arms and legs. Milan threw himself on him.

"Stop it! You're hurting them. Let me do it."

He knelt down and very gently, as if tending the severely wounded, raised one of the heads and rested it against his forearm, slid his other hand under the waist of the dummy, and stood up, gazing tenderly down at the disjointed body. The sight of so much solicitude had reduced Bonami to silence. Milan turned to Idris and put the little boy in his arms. Then he stooped down to the second dummy.

"How much do you want for them?" he asked Bonami.

"Oh, those two, you can have them! They're rejects."

"Yes, they've suffered a great deal. I'm going to give them some new hair and eyelashes. Repaint their cheeks and lips. And their clothes! A whole trousseau to collect!" he sighed happily, imagining long hours of tranquil work on his new children.

Parisians may well have the reputation of not being surprised by anything; nevertheless, these two men solemnly walking along, each cradling in his arms a ragged, disfigured boy whose legs were dangling in the void, did not always pass unremarked as they went up and then crossed the Boulevard Barbès and turned into the Rue de la Goutte-d'Or. For some, surprise was compounded by doubt: were they injured children, corpses, or dummies? Some people looked around, shocked. Others laughed. Idris thought about his camel, and how he had crossed Paris in search of an abattoir. This time the journey was shorter. Milan had stopped outside a dilapidated apartment block, temporarily shored up by wooden beams.

"This is it," he said, pushing the door with his knee.

They went up a dark staircase whose wrought-iron handrail

showed that it had known better days, and stopped on the second floor. A poster on the door merrily celebrated the puppet show in the Luxembourg Gardens. The room they entered smelled of glue and varnish. A plank on two trestles did duty as a workbench or operating table. And anyway, it was occupied by a big articulated doll made of wood, and littered with brushes, spatulas, tubes, scrapers, and bottles. Milan knelt down and deposited his burden on a camp bed. Then he relieved Idris of the other dummy, which he put down beside the first. He stood up, and granted himself a moment of tender contemplation.

"You might think they were twin brothers," he said dreamily. "When I was that age there were two in my class. They spent their whole time making people take one for the other. Separately, each was a completely normal, ordinary boy. And then all of a sudden the anomaly appeared: you were seeing double. Their absolute resemblance was staggering, but there was also something comic about it. Exactly like dummies: a mixture of anguish and fun. And in any case, dummies and twins are close relations, since a dummy necessarily conjures up a procedure that enables the same model to be mass-produced."

They took a few steps.

"I only have two rooms. This is the workshop, and that's the bedroom."

He raised the curtain separating the two rooms and stood aside to let Idris pass, as if to allow him to take the shock on his own. The room looked like the scene of a massacre, or perhaps the Ogre's larder. True, it was just possible to make out a couch tucked away in a corner with a bedside light. But piles of torsos, bundles of arms, sheaves of legs meticulously lined up against the walls were reminiscent of a special kind of charnel house; very clean, very dry, but made even more ambiguous by the rows of smiling heads with pink cheeks occupying the shelves.

"Can you sleep here?" Idris asked in amazement.

Milan didn't answer, being totally absorbed by the presence of these fragmented little men. He picked up a torso and tapped its smooth surface.

"Can you hear? It rings hollow. It's a plaster shell. I like plaster. It's a friable, porous material that's sensitive to the slightest humidity; it's fragile, but easy to produce, to paint, and to idealize. What I would really like best would be to live in a world of plaster. Whereas the nude in painting and sculpture is related to anatomy and physiology, you know in advance that the dummy exists in a vacuum and contains nothing. You don't dissect a dummy. The child who opens up its celluloid doll to see what's inside it is an idiot, or a potential sadist. He will be disappointed when he doesn't find anything. The dummy has no inner being. It's a totally superficial character, devoid of the more or less repugnant secrets hidden under the skin of the living. The ideal, in short!"

They went back into the first room.

"But what do you do with these dummies?"

"What do I do with them? After all, I could easily be quite happy just to live with them. What do collectors do with their collections? They surround themselves with them, they handle their pieces, they dust them. I look after my little men. Sometimes I make one, by assembling his arms, legs, and head on a torso. This can produce very touching disproportions. Those are great moments. Paternity . . . And in any case, I'm not the only one. I have correspondents who share my passion. That's to say . . . more or less. Most of them are only interested in women, or at best in little girls. We write to each other. Occasionally we exchange our finds. But they have no flair. They tell me they've got a marvel, I rush off to see it, and it's absolutely nothing. I'm the only one who knows! In the summer we go down to Provence. My parents still live in the Lubéron district. They run a home for delicate children who need medical supervision. That's where it all began for me when I was at the divine age. When I got older I was rejected into outer darkness. I've put up a little shelter in a nearby field to house my little men. I take them by car. My little Citroën 2CV is cram-full of dummies, the ones I've collected and repaired during the winter. We drive slowly. We do the journey in several stages. We're a terrific success, I assure you! The thing that amazes people is that I myself am made of flesh and blood. They seem to expect the car to be driven by a dummy. Actually, they're right. I ought to be a dummy too. That would bring me closer to them. When we arrive in Provence, it's marvelous. The little men I bring with me come from the North of France. I show them the olive groves and the lavender fields. I observe the happy amazement on their painted faces. When we get to my parents' house the children come flocking around us. They observe my traveling companions with interest. Most of them don't understand. They're afraid. But I always notice one or two who are going to enter into my game. And anyway, it's easy to spot them; they're the ones who most resemble my little dummies. They have round cheeks, almond-shaped eyes, neat blond hair with a part on one side, something of the superhuman, of the inhuman, which is unmistakable. These children will join my little troupe, they will merge indiscriminately with my little men. A day or two later, the party begins. It lasts all through the summer. We take possession of the scrubland and the limestone hills bristling with evergreen oaks. We play football, battledore and shuttlecock, blindman's buff. We go on picnics. For our siesta, when the day is at its hottest, I make a bed of cushions under a canvas. In the evening of the thirteenth of July there are fireworks, dancing, and a candlelit supper. The summer holidays are bliss. Incidentally, that's the title of a book of photographs I'm preparing. Because I take color photographs of all these parties with my little men."

"You photograph them!"

Idris had not been able to hold back this exclamation.

"Yes, of course; it's a tradition. You always photograph important occasions, christenings, communions, marriages, boys leaving to join the army. I compose tableaux with my little men, and just for fun I include one or two live boys. The party begins as something local and ephemeral, but through photography it becomes universal and eternal. It's a consecration."

"You photograph dummies!" Idris repeated, sensing all that was subtly maleficent in this operation.

"Yes, but with a bit of landscape, real landscape, real trees, real rocks. And like that, you see, there's a sort of mutual contamination between my boy dolls and the landscape. The reality of the landscape brings the dummies to life much more intensely than any shopwindow display. But it's the reverse that really matters: my dummies throw doubt on the landscape. Thanks to them, the trees just slightly—not completely, only slightly—seem to be made of cardboard, and part of the sky seems to be just a backcloth. As for the dummies, since they themselves are already images, their photo is the image of an image, and this has the effect of doubling their dissolving power. The result is an impression of a waking dream, a genuine hallucination. It is, absolutely, reality being undermined at its very foundations by image."

Idris hadn't been listening for a long time.

"If you don't need me anymore," he said, "I'll go back to Tati's. I need a pair of dungarees for work."

"You can stay and have lunch with me if you like, but I must warn you that I'm a vegetarian."

"What's a vegetarian?"

"I don't eat meat or fish."

"At home in Tabelbala, we only eat vegetables."

"Yes, but that's from necessity. With me, it's my choice. Meat is man, fish is woman, two things I've eliminated from my life."

Later he returned to the subject of their meeting and to Bonami's proposition to Idris.

"He wants to have a mold taken of me to make African dummies. For his shopwindows," Idris explained.

"He suggested that to you?"

Milan looked at him, seeming both startled and delighted.

"Yes, yes, but I'm not sure I'll go!"

"You must go, d'you hear me, you absolutely must go! It's a fantastic experience."

"Go yourself, if you think it's so interesting!"

"In the first place, I'm not the Maghrebi type. You saw, we were both there. It's you he wants. And then, for me, it's too late. I ought to have done it fifteen years ago. When I was ten, though, I was just a little peasant in the Lubéron, and not only did no one make molds of me, but the rare photos they took of me at the time are dreadful. There was only one compensation for my poverty—my mother never threw anything away. When I'd worn out a shirt or a pair of trousers, she put them away for goodness knows what hypothetical use. And that was how I found a whole trunkful of children's clothes from the sixties in our attic. It's my treasure trove. It's only as a very rare exception that I bring it out to dress some of my favorite little men, and then only for great, for very great occasions."

Idris was not interested in hearing what these great occasions consisted of. He was eating some rice with tomatoes and onion puree, and trying to imagine where he was going to be led by this business of the molding, which he had a feeling he was not going to escape. He saw himself multiplied tenfold, a hundredfold, reduced to an infinity of wax dolls frozen in ridiculous postures under the eyes of the crowd massed in front of the Tati shopwindows. How the metamorphosis would take place, he so far had no idea.

"You *must* go," Milan repeated before he let him go, patting him on the shoulder with an encouraging smile. "And don't forget—come back and tell me all about it."

Twenty-three

HE DID GO. One morning Bonami, who had arranged to meet him in the Boulevard de la Chapelle, picked him up and drove off in the direction of the Avenue Jean-Jaurès. The laboratories of the Glyptoplastic Company were in Pantin, on the premises of the wax-modeling workshops formerly used by Charles-Louis Auzoux. There, more than a century earlier, the famous Saint-Aubin anatomist had founded a strange factory that supplied all the faculties of medicine in France and the rest of the world with anatomical models made of wax. They could be totally dismantled and their internal organs, scrupulously reproduced even down to their color, could be removed and handled by students. After the war Glypto had modernized these techniques and extended their scope. It supplied the Paris waxworks, cinema production companies, display artists, illusionists, and even some undertakers, who could thus offer their customers a life-sized effigy of the dear departed.

At the Glypto premises the visitor was confronted with a somewhat heterogeneous sample of its products, both from the prodigious past and from more recent days. Some of these, hanging on the walls like hunting trophies and dating from the time of Dr. Auzoux, were a pair of vermilion lungs joined by their trachea, a metallic-brown liver with its portal vein, its hepatic veins, and its lymph vessels, and, for no apparent reason, an engraving illustrating eight pink noses with the description of their various types written in a beautiful round hand: straight (Greek), flat (Negroid), hooked (Red Indian), drooping, snub, aquiline, Bourbon, and retroussé. There was also an assortment of flexible, pustulous masks, artificial hands with their fingers eaten away, and a shirtfront made to look like a woman's torso with the breasts consumed by a purulent chancre; their presence was explained by the requirements of a film in which certain sequences took place in a leper hospital. But there were also busts with smiling faces and dazzling teeth for hairdressers' windows, a ballerina whose fleshy curves were veiled by a dusty tutu, and, survivors of an updating at the waxworks, a Vincent Auriol, President of the Republic, and an Édouard Herriot, secretary of the Rādical Socialist Party. In a nearby room a young sculptor, surrounded by the entire Glypto team, was swaddling a life-sized Christ which had just been taken out of its mold and which he was about to take away in his van. Not knowing how to solder tin cans together to make abstract compositions, he had been taken unawares by a commission to make a 180-cm-high Christ on the cross for a recently restored church. In order not to lose the commission, he had come to Glypto, and as an economy measure had decided to use himself as a model, so that it was his own molding that he was preparing to crucify.

"No one could carry his professional conscience to greater lengths," he was explaining to the others as he wrapped up his double, "but if I had any kind of mystical vocation, I don't know where this sort of jape might not lead me."

The arrival of Bonami and Idris created a diversion. They were taken to the molding laboratory. The molding cell was like a narrow phone booth made of Plexiglas. It was there that the sculptor, two days before, had been put on the cross before being covered with paste. A steep, narrow flight of steps gave access to the upper floor. In an electrically heated vat, 700 liters of alginate—a slimy substance formed by the gum of certain brown algae on contact with water—was kept at a temperature of 25 degrees Celsius. Through a sluice gate communicating with the ground floor, this mixture was poured into the molding cell. Two other vats were ready for use. In one, 60 liters (the equivalent of Idris's weight) of polyester resin, diluted with 50 percent water, was kept in emulsion by a mixer, whose drone filled the room. The other contained the 80 liters of catalyst that would be added to the alginate at the last moment to harden it. A hoist, fixed to a beam on the roof and ending in the bar of a trapeze, was used to pull the model out of the hardening mass of the alginate.

All these explanations by the chief technician, of which Idris didn't understand a word, completed his terror. He was assured, however, that he would remain in the cell for only a few minutes, just long enough for the alginate to become doughy, like pastry. After that, the polyester resin would be poured into the pocket formed by his body, and then, after being cooled for thirty-six hours, it would produce a matrix in his likeness and of his weight. This matrix would be used to make a cast-aluminum mold, from which they would make an unlimited number of polyethylene or PVC dummies. First, though, they needed to take an impression of his face. This, in short, would be a slight foretaste of the modeling of his body.

They sat him, bare-chested, at a table on which there was a bowl of alginate. An assistant poured in the catalyst and checked how the paste was setting. As there was no difficulty involved in removing the model, they could wait until the paste had set harder, and thus reduce the duration of the immersion. Idris took a deep breath and plunged his face into the bowl. A heavy hand on the back of his neck pressed him down into it up to his ears. He had been advised to hold out as long as he could. After about a minute he straightened up, half asphyxiated. But the mixture had set more quickly than expected, and he left his eyelashes and eyebrows behind in it.

"They'll grow again," one of the assistants joked. "But as you see, we could sell our stuff as depilatory wax."

Next he had to strip completely and go into the cell. This was where Bonami's artistic sense came into play, because the dummies were going to be rigid and would all be in the attitude adopted by Idris in the paste. This was a long and meticulous business. His right leg had to move forward slightly without leaving the left one in a stiff attitude. His torso had to be slightly twisted, and his arms must be held in a vague gesture of unselfconscious welcome. The whole effect must reconcile movement and balance, elegance and naturalness, grace and virility. The Glypto technicians had other worries. There was a chance that after the model had been removed the amorphous mass of 800 kilos of alginate might collapse and close in on the impression of his body. So Idris's body was surrounded with an armature of about a dozen long metal rods with steel rings, whose function was to strengthen the paste. In their first experiments, it had happened that they had been unable to extract the model from the enormous, sticky matrix. Between Idris's toes they placed narrow tubes connected to a bottle of compressed air. The air forced in would slightly distend the impression and facilitate the release of the model.

The Glypto people knew from experience that the mental and moral resistance of the model is an essential factor in the success of the operation. They made Bonami stop pestering Idris. They wanted to get it over with. The chief technician got up on a stepladder, in order to be able to look down into the cell. His head was within a few centimeters of that of Idris, who was contorted in his dummy's pose. His hand was on the sluice-gate lever.

"You all right, pal? Here we go, then!"

With a whoomph, a greenish dung came crashing down on Idris's feet. Then the sluice spewed down the viscous torrent of the alginate, into which the catalyst was gradually amalgamated. The level rose very rapidly up Idris's body. It was soft, warm, in no way unpleasant. He began to feel some distress, though, when the paste reached his chest. He inflated his lungs, as he had been advised, to expand the matrix, which was suffocating him. But the terrifying thing was the hardening of the paste, which, starting from his feet, was now closing in over the whole of his body. When the level had reached his chin, the chief technician closed the sluice and let no more than a trickle run down into the cell.

"Don't be afraid," he said, "I'll get your mouth, but I'll stop before it reaches your nostrils."

Idris had shut his eyes. He felt as if he had stopped breathing, as if his heart had stopped beating. Before the green sludge completely gagged him, he uttered one word.

"What did he say?" asked Bonami.

"I don't know. It was like a name. Something like "Ibrahim."

"Even so, we mustn't let him croak!"

"Don't tempt fate! We've got to wait at least three minutes, though, to give the paste time to set properly. Otherwise, we'll have to do the whole thing again."

"Just enough time to boil an egg!"

"Very funny!"

The seconds dragged by interminably. The chief technician kept dipping his index finger into the alginate to judge its consistency.

"I think that'll do," he finally said. "Pump in the compressed air."

There was a slight hiss, then a profound belch. The air forced its way up Idris's body.

"Trapeze!" the chief ordered.

He had freed Idris's arms, and he helped him close his hands on the bar of the trapeze. On the upper floor, two men tugged on the hoist rope with all their strength. Slowly, the trapeze rose. Two men were now keeping Idris's hands clenched on the bar. The mass of alginate released the naked body, producing terrible farting, sucking, and swallowing noises.

"You might think you were watching the birth of a child," Bonami declared.

"It's more like a calf being pulled out of a cow's belly!"

The men on the first floor let go of the rope and helped Idris to his feet. Naked, his body shining with a slimy varnish, he staggered like a shipwrecked sailor.

"Take him to the shower and give him his gear while I pour the resin in."

An hour later, Bonami drove Idris back to the Rue Myrha. He was bubbling over with enthusiasm.

"It was a bit tough, eh, but what a fantastic adventure! The birth of a child, yes, it was the birth of a child! And in less than a month there'll be about twenty Idrises, all as alike as twin brothers, peopling my windows and counters. And while we're on the subject, I've had an idea that I'd like to put to you. It's this: why don't you learn to act the robot? We dress you like the other dummies, your twin brothers. We make you up so that your face, your hair, your hands, look artificial, if you see what I mean. And you, stiff as a poker in the shopwindow, you make a few awkward, jerky movements. It's already been done, mind you. It's a surefire success. Morning and evening, there are crowds milling around the window. It's quite easy, but more tiring than you might think. The hardest thing is the eyes. You mustn't blink. Yes, you mustn't close your lids. The eye suffers a bit at first from desiccation, but you get used to it. What do you say? Think over my proposition. It would be very well paid. And come and see me about it."

Twenty-four

THE NEXT FEW DAYS, exhausted by his painful experiences, Idris hardly left the hostel in the Rue Myrha. He felt a need to protect himself from the outside world, and wanted to avoid the pitfalls and mirages that appeared beneath his feet. The hostel was dormant all afternoon, and only came to life after six in the evening, when the men came back from work. Isidore took advantage of this to take a look around the rooms, using his master key. He made a mental note of the remarks he would make to the occupants the same evening. Some rooms were in meticulous order. Others, on the contrary, displayed provocative filth. Isidore knew his people. These men, uprooted from the family life of their remote villages, sometimes didn't even know that clothes and dishes don't simply wash themselves, or that it isn't advisable to break a window to make it easier to throw your slops out into the street. Old Isidore watched over them, paternal, authoritarian, and with the assurance gained from long experience. Some elderly immigrants were already drawing a pension and had dug themselves into the hostel for good, although it was never intended to be an old people's home. These were Isidore's favorite tenants, they were the quietest, the tidiest, the easiest. They gathered together in the common room around the clay kanoun on which the tea was brewing and played dominoes or kharbaga, exchanging rare remarks. Idris sometimes joined them in these idle hours and together, with sporadic allusions, they evoked the Algeria of their youth.

This old brigade, together with the immigrants of longest standing, formed the group of those who listened to the radio, which was separated by a generation—or even two—from the television fiends. Television was image, was modern life, the French language, or even a window onto the American way of life. Whereas the radio—which you could only hear at certain hours, and sometimes only with your ear glued to the set—was Cairo, Tripoli, or Algiers, the Arabic language, political speeches, and above all the Koran and traditional music. Idris, bruised by his misadventures, sought the company of his kindly elders, who were glad to welcome him and who initiated him into the invisible, crackling world of the ionosphere. He gradually came to understand that a defense against the maleficent power of the image, which seduces the eye, might be found in the acoustic sign, which alerts the ear. He found a passionate guide in the person of a tailor of Egyptian origin. Mohammed Amouzine had been in France since the end of the war. Fate had prevented him from returning to his village, where a whole tribe was dependent on the money he sent home. But he was consumed by nostalgia. "The Egyptian has been attached to the land of the Nile for seven thousand years, and he, of all the peasants in the whole Arab world, has the least natural gift for the nomadic life," he explained. "Nothing is more repugnant to him than to leave his country." He had lived on tenterhooks, his hands folded over his Koran, his ear glued to his radio, through the first defeat of the Egyptian Army by Israel in 1948, the fall of King Farouk in 1952, the nationalization of the Suez Canal followed by the cowardly triple Franco-Anglo-Israeli attack in 1956, the Six-Day War in

1967, and, most of all, the death of the Bikbashi, President Nasser, on September 28, 1970, and his grandiose funeral. He explained to Idris the somber, stirring beauty of the political speeches broadcast daily by *The Voice of the Arabs,* their declamatory triumphalism, so little justified by the facts, but so much in keeping with the potential power of the Islamic world.

But it was above all the sublime voice of Oum Kalsoum that aroused his passionate enthusiasm. Mohammed Amouzine, the little tailor from Cairo, could talk forever about "the Nightingale of the Delta," "the Star of the Orient," the singer who was finally quite simply known as "the Lady" (as Sett). Because he had been born in the same year—1904—near Simballawen in a province of the Egyptian Rif, Dakahliya, which was where she too came from, he felt as if he were her fellow villager, almost her brother. Dressed as a boy as an austerity measure, she was already singing at marriages at the age of eight. She was paid with a few cakes, before falling asleep exhausted in her father's arms. She was not accompanied by any instruments, for the voice is the sole musical instrument given by God. The fame of this Bedouin child, who embellished family celebrations with her praise of the Prophet, was constantly growing. There was a catastrophe, however, the day when for the first time her photo appeared in a newspaper. This was the start of her glory, but to her father it represented ineffaceable dishonor. From then on, all her life she had had to fight against photographers thirsting to pry into her private life and reveal its most trivial images. Oum Kalsoum's public was almost exclusively masculine, and she was a woman without a man. (Quite late in life she married the doctor who had been treating her.) She saw herself as the bride of the whole Arab people, a sort of madonna, a vestal of the nation which saw her art as a mission that was both sentimental and patriotic. "It's like a political meeting," husbands would tell their wives, to explain why they went alone to listen to the singer. And besides, *kalsoum* means "banner," and on stage she always held a huge handkerchief in her right hand, which she flourished like a veil, like a pennon. It was her symbol, but also her refuge, the confidant of her tears and her sweat.

Oum Kalsoum's eyes had been made protuberant by goiter, and she appeared with them hidden behind big dark glasses; with a scarf tied over her hair, for through Arab atavism she felt more at her ease with her head covered; and with her plump hand waving her handkerchief. She was the first to have the audacity to reject literary Arabic and to sing on the radio in the Egyptian dialect. And the miracle was that she managed to make herself understood throughout the Arab world. When one of her recitals was broadcast live on the radio, suddenly, at the same moment, the streets and markets were seen to empty in Cairo, Casablanca, Tunis, Beirut, Damascus, Khartoum, and Riyadh. The crowds acclaimed her with extravagant words: "You belong to us. You are the fiancée of my life. Since I have known you I have become deaf, I hear only your voice; I have become mute, I speak only of you!"

Henceforth, this voice was inseparable from the life of the nation. She was the soul of Egypt and of the entire Arab world. A saying went the rounds: "How are things in Egypt? Fine: three days of football, three days of Oum Kalsoum, one day of meat." On July 22, 1952, a group of young officers put an end to thousands of years of foreign subjection. For the first time since the Pharaohs, Egypt was independent. But General Neguib and Colonel Nasser could not do without the influence of Oum Kalsoum. The Revolution had to be crowned with a recital given by the Star of the Orient. Neguib and Nasser were in the front row. And when, after the disasters of the Six-Day War in June 1967, the desperate Bikbashi announced his resignation, once again Oum Kalsoum's voice was heard, obliging him to stay on:

Rise up and listen to my heart, for I am the people.
Stay; you are our rampart, our defense.
Stay; you are the last hope of all the people.

You are our well-being, our light; you are our patience
in the face of fate.

You are the victor and the victory.
Stay; you embody the love of our nation,
The love, the artery of the people![1]

On March 21, 1969, all the necessary conditions seemed to
have been achieved for Abdul Salam Jallud and Muammar al-
Qaddafi to be able to overthrow King Idris and take power in
Libya. All the conditions save one: that evening, the Nightingale of the Delta was singing in Benghazi! A national event
incompatible with a coup d'état. The conspirators could not be
anywhere other than among the audience, acclaiming their
idol. They had to call off the revolution and wait nearly six
months—until September 1—for the conditions once more to
be favorable.

Amouzine never tired of recalling the two memorable con-
certs she had given in Paris, at the Olympia, on November 15
and 17, 1967. On the fifteenth, the crowd massed on the pavement in the Boulevard des Capucines was immense, and gave
him little hope of being able to get in. True, there were disrep-
utable individuals hanging around offering black-market tickets, but their price was way beyond the means of a tailor with a
family to support. This was when fate miraculously intervened
in his favor. He noticed a blind man making his way through
the pedestrians, slowly and gently sweeping the ground with
his white stick. He was an old Arab, wearing a turban and a
djellaba. Amouzine's immediate reaction was quite disinter-
ested; he rushed up to help him. But he soon realized how he
could turn his generosity to account. Taking the blind man by
the arm, he said quickly, "Come with me, I'll get you in."
Then he forced his way through the crowd in the foyer, pushing the old man in front of him and repeating, "Make way
please, make way please!" In all countries in the world, but

[1] Words by Saleh Gaoudat, quoted in *Oum Kalsoum* by Ysabel Saïah (Denoël).

more especially among a public the majority of whom are African, the blind inspire respectful fear. Amouzine and his protégé soon found themselves in the theater, and then in the front row, right up against the footlights. It was a real miracle, and the tailor still laughed with joy when he recalled it. But there was a second miracle—and how much more profound, more meaningful, more touching it was!

The curtain rose. The little orchestra that traditionally accompanied Oum Kalsoum was already in place, and as usual played a long prelude. It was a sinuous melody, outlined by the violins, then taken up by the ganouns and lutes, and finally emphasized by the electronic organ. Then the singer appeared, encircled in the pencil of light coming from a spot, and silently walked up to the mike. She raised her head as if inspired, and let her long scarf hang down inertly from her hand. No cries, no applause, no display of feeling greeted her long-awaited arrival. She lowered her head a little and seemed to be scrutinizing the dark, gaping maw of the auditorium. Oum Kalsoum had been on relatively few tours outside the Arab countries. She was so profoundly rooted in her deltaic land that she always felt a certain repugnance at venturing into the West represented by the European capitals and the great American cities. This could be felt in her attitude as she faced this Paris audience. She was visibly searching the obscure crowd for a face, a gaze, to reassure her and to transmit the current between the public and herself. She found one. But it was a sightless gaze. In the front row she saw the blind man in his turban and djellaba and with his white stick. She murmured in an imperceptible voice, "I shall be singing for *you.*" Did anyone other than the blind man hear? No one knows for sure. But the old man shivered. No longer darkened by his blindness, his face lit up in a smile. He listened passionately. She was singing for *him!* And by his side, the little tailor who had witnessed the miracle, a miracle in which he had played his part, remained silent, transfixed with joy and wonderment.

"When we came out," he told Idris, "the crowd made way

for us with respect. I couldn't help asking the blind man how he imagined Oum Kalsoum. I was so bemused, I must even have asked him how he saw her. But as if my question was not at all incongruous, he had no hesitation in answering it. "Green!" he told me. This man who had been blind from birth saw our national singer as a color, the color green! And he added: 'Her voice has as many nuances as all the green in nature, and green is the color of the Prophet.' "

Having reported this remark, Amouzine fell silent, and smiled at Idris. Would this boy, who was so young, understand that the word can be sufficiently powerful to make a blind man see, that the sign can be sufficiently rich to evoke the color green in his darkened head?

Idris had not seen Oum Kalsoum any more than the blind man had, and there was no way his imagination could be fired by the press clipping that Amouzine kept tucked away in his wallet, which merely gave the impression of a fat lady with a heavy face hidden under thick dark glasses. But he listened to her for hours on end, and very gradually the memory of Zett Zobeida imposed itself on his mind. It was the same voice, a little too deep for a woman, the voice of the young Bedouin boy whose appearance Oum Kalsoum had adopted at the beginning of her career, with sensual intonations of heartrending sadness. Then Idris remembered the dancer's shiny black belly, the lipless mouth through which the whole of the modestly veiled body was expressed. It was the same perfectly distinct articulation, the same emphatic pronunciation, the words being detached according to the rules of Koranic diction, and also the same modulated repetition, the tireless return of the same verse repeated with different intonation to the point of vertigo, to the point of hypnosis. The dragonfly that is a skit and that thwarts the tricks of death, the cricket that is a script and that tells the secret of life . . .

It was also Amouzine who introduced Idris to the master calligrapher Abd Al Ghafari.

Twenty-five

If what you have to say is not more beautiful
than silence,
Then keep quiet!

CALLIGRAPHED on the door lintel in the angular, geometric Kufic script, this injunction had been Idris's first lesson. The fact is that the master, Abd Al Ghafari, advised all his pupils not to open their mouths during the first three-quarters of an hour of the lesson.

In the little room where the ink was made, another text was to be read on the wall. It was the saying of the Prophet which asserts the absolute contrast between the wisdom of Islam and the cult of suffering and death peculiar to Christianity:

There is more truth in the ink of scholars than in the blood
of martyrs.

Idris learned how to make this scholars' ink. To half a liter of water you had to add five grams of salt, two hundred and fifty grams of gum arabic, thirty grams of nut gall roasted and then powdered, forty grams of ferrous sulfate, and thirty grams of honey. Heat gently for two hours, stirring from time to time, then add twenty grams of lampblack and continue heating for another hour. Finally, strain the ink through a very fine filter.

He also practiced cutting reeds, for the calligrapher must make his implement himself and use it only once. The length of the reed pen is one span—namely, the distance between the extremities of the thumb and the little finger when the fingers are outstretched. You press the tip of the reed down onto a small cutting plate made of ivory, mother-of-pearl, or shell. Sliced at an oblique angle, the reed terminates in a nib covering an oval hollow. The nib is slit, not in its center, but at four-fifths of its width. The slit must be short for heavy hands, longer for light hands. There is a reed for each script—Riqa, Fasi, Kufic, Naskhi, Thuluth, Divani, Jazm—and as many reeds as there are thicknesses of characters.

But these peaceful, monotonous little tasks were really only the prelude to the fundamental act, the delineation of the letter. From his very first calligraphy, Idris found himself plunged back into the time beyond measure when he had lived without knowing it in Tabelbala. He now understood that those vast stretches of duration were a gift of his childhood, and that from now on he would regain them by study, practice, and disinterestedness. And besides, the faculty given to the calligrapher to lengthen certain letters horizontally introduces silences into the line, zones of calm and repose, which are the desert itself.

It is not only his hand that the pupil has to master, it is also his breathing. Idris learned by heart this page from the master calligrapher Hassan Massoudy on the interdependence of breathing and writing:

The capacity of the calligrapher to hold his breath is reflected in the quality of his execution. Normally, one breathes without method. But when calligraphing, one cannot breathe in and out no matter when. Throughout his apprenticeship the calligrapher will learn to suspend his respiration, and to use a break in the delineation of a letter to take another breath. An upstroke or a downstroke will not be the same if one breathes in or out while making it. When the stroke is long, if the line is to remain pure one must suspend one's breathing, so that it does not alter the movement. Before calligraphing a letter or a word, one must foresee the places where one is going to be able to take another breath, and at the same time to replenish the pen with ink. These breaks are made in precise, codified places, even if one is still capable of holding one's breath and some ink still remains in the reed. These breaks, therefore, serve for the replenishment both of air and of ink. Calligraphers who perpetuate the traditional methods do not like to use metallic fountain pens, for they provide an uninterrupted flow of ink which renders such mastery useless, and deprives the calligrapher of the pleasure of feeling the weight of time.

As Arabic is written with the right hand and from right to left, care must be taken to avoid passing the hand over a newly written line. In fact, the hand must be like a ballerina and dance lightly over the parchment, not weigh down on it like a farm laborer with his plow.

Calligraphy abhors the void. The whiteness of the page attracts it, as an atmospheric depression attracts the winds and raises a storm. A storm of signs that come and alight on the page in clouds, like birds of ink on a field of snow. The black signs, lined up in bellicose cohorts, their beaks raised, their crops swollen, their wings folded, march from line to line, and then reassemble in corollas, in rosettes, in choirs, in skillful symmetry.

The sculptor's chisel liberates the girl, the athlete, or the horse from the block of marble. In the same way, signs are all prisoners of the ink and the inkwell. The reed pen liberates them, and releases them on the page. Calligraphy is liberation.

More than once in his remarks the master, Abd Al Ghafari, had alluded to an exemplary tale in which, according to him, was to be found the last word on his teaching, and all the wisdom of calligraphy. This was "The Legend of the Blond Queen." But his young apprentices had to be capable of grasping its meaning and turning it to their advantage. These Moslem adolescents, submerged in the big occidental city, were subjected to all the assaults of the effigy, the idol, and the figure. Three words to designate the same servitude. The effigy is a door bolt, the idol a prison, the figure a lock. Only one key can remove these chains: the sign. The image is always retrospective. It is a mirror turned toward the past. There is no purer image than the tombstone profile, the death mask, the lid of the sarcophagus. But alas, it exerts its omnipotent fascination on simple, ill-prepared souls. A prison is not merely bars, it is also a roof. A bolt prevents me from getting out, but it also protects me against the monsters of the night. A figure carved in stone tempts one to a vertiginous dive into the shadows of an immemorial past. The most vulgar form of this sort of opium is to be found in the cinemas. There, in the depths of darkened auditoria, men and women, sunk side by side in uncomfortable seats, remain frozen for hours on end in the hypnotic contemplation of a vast, dazzling screen that occupies the whole of their visual field. And the dead images restlessly moving on this scintillating surface penetrate them to the heart, and they have not the slightest defense against them.

The image is indeed the opium of the Occident. The sign is spirit, the image is matter. Calligraphy is the algebra of the soul traced by the most spiritualized organ of the body, its right hand. It is the celebration of the invisible by the visible. The arabesque manifests the presence of the desert in the mosque. Through the arabesque, the infinite is deployed in the finite. For the desert is pure space, freed from the vicissitudes of time. It is God without man. The calligrapher, who in the solitude of his cell takes possession of the desert by peopling it with signs, escapes from the misery of the past, from the agony of the future, and from the tyranny of other men. Alone, he converses with God, in a climate of eternity.

Evening after evening, Idris thus made his way toward recovery, listening to the lessons of the master, Abd Al Ghafari, and regenerating his hands, coarsened by his rough daytime jobs.

Until the day when he and a few others were invited by the master to sit around him and hear "The Legend of the Blond Queen."

Twenty-six

The Blond Queen

ONCE UPON A TIME there was a queen, and this queen was so radiantly beautiful that men could not see her without loving her passionately. One particularity, rare and strange in those southern countries, no doubt contributed to this woman's dangerous charm: she was as blond as ripe corn, and this requires an explanation, for her parents' hair was of the darkest jet black.

They had known each other since they were very young, and they belonged to two great rival neighboring families who hated each other. They could only meet in secret, and their meetings usually took place in an abandoned palm grove invaded by the sand. But one night, when they had made love even more passionately than on the other nights, they lingered on, and the first ray of the rising sun caressed the entwined couple at the very moment when they were conceiving their first child, and this constitutes a grave infringement of the rules of decency. But should we not forgive those who are constrained by the stupidity and hatred of others to make love under the palm trees and the sky, like the birds and beasts? Now, no one in this country was unaware of the punishment meted out to those who make love in full daylight: the solar child is condemned to be born blond, to be of accusatory, indecent, bewitching blondness . . .

This was the case, then, with their daughter, who sowed scandal around her and reaped contempt, long before she was able to understand the reason for her malediction. Yet the more she grew, the more resplendent became her beauty, the more dazzling her blondness. And what had to happen happened. The king's eldest son, having caught a fleeting glimpse of her, fell in love with her and sorely distressed his family and the court by demanding for his bride this bastard with the obscene hair. The celebrations attending their marriage were all the more magnificent in that they coincided with the coronation of the prince. Indeed, it was not until he became king that he was able to conquer the resistance of all the notables to what they considered a dreadful misalliance.

Alas, the young royal couple's happiness was of short duration. When the new king's younger brother, who was a page at a foreign court, saw his sister-in-law for the first time, he conceived an immeasurable passion for her. And he went so far as to kill his brother, not from the base motive of taking his place on the throne and in his bed, but in an access of mad jealousy, so that his brother would not touch the blond queen.

She, cruelly wounded by this fratricide of which she knew herself to be the cause, rejected every idea of remarriage and decided to reign alone. And to put an end to the ravages exerted by her blond beauty, she covered her head and face with a veil, which she only removed in her private apartments, and only in the presence of her female attendants. As the sovereign is at all times and in all places a model for his subjects, the custom was established in the kingdom that women never went out unless concealed behind a veil.

It was this custom that a young painter named Ismaïl turned to account in order to carry out an audacious plan. He had convinced himself that his vocation could not come to fruition unless he managed to paint the portrait of the queen. He bribed one of the maids in the gynaeceum and took her place, his face hidden under a veil, and thus, day after day, he was able to feast his eyes on the beauty of the queen. Whenever he had a free moment he shut himself up in a small room and applied himself with passion to the work of his life.

But this work was to be the only one, for Ismaïl realized that he would never be able to paint anything else. Furthermore, he was mad with hopeless love, and he hanged himself beside his portrait.

The queen grew old, her hair became white, and she died. But her portrait preserved—intact, and even mysteriously enhanced—the dangerous charm of her features. It passed from hand to hand, exciting an absolute but hopeless passion in men's hearts. From time to time it was exhibited in a room in the palace beside the treasures accumulated by generations of tyrants. The steward was alarmed by the ardent love letters daily addressed by unknown men to the blond queen. One morning the attendants were found murdered. Thieves had broken in through the roof and made their way into the gallery containing the treasures. They had left the silver-gilt table services, however, and the precious stones and golden medals. Only the portrait of the queen had disappeared.

Two years later, a traveler crossing the nearby desert discovered the corpses of two men. As they still had their weapons in their hands, it was easy to see that they had killed each other. As for the cause of this brawl, it was there, radiating maleficent blondness. It was the portrait of the queen.

The traveler, who was a pious man, buried the desiccated corpses, said a prayer for them, and continued on his way. But he had added the portrait to his baggage. His name was Abder, he was a member of a strict sect, and he sold icons and pious images in the souks in the town. Yet he was careful not to exhibit the blond queen in his shop. He hung the portrait in the conjugal bedroom, telling his wife that he did not know who was its model; the truth, in short. Ayesha was at first reassured, but she soon realized the perturbation this image caused in her husband's heart. She was too familiar with the weight of his gaze not to notice the somber flame burning in his eyes whenever he looked at the painted woman. So she determined to destroy the maleficent image. One day when an engraver was working in the shop she appropriated his bottle of vitriol and broke it on the queen's face. Mysteriously, no trace appeared on the portrait. But Ayesha, on the other hand, was horribly burned about the face, and by evening was hideously disfigured. She swore to everyone that it was her husband who had thrown the vitriol in her face during a quarrel. Abder, taken before the tribunal of his sect, refused to defend himself. To do so he would have had to take it upon himself to accuse Ayesha and reveal the secret of the painted queen, which was beyond his strength. His silence was taken for a confession, he was condemned to have all his property confiscated and to end his days in a monastery.

The painted queen disappeared for a few years, but it is possible that she played a part in numerous mysterious affairs that remained unexplained.

A long time later, the strange behavior of the king of a neighboring country was causing concern to his court. He had a secret room to which no one was admitted. But every day he was seen to shut himself up in it and to remain there for several hours, sometimes for a whole night. When he came out he was pale, haggard, and they could see from his eyes that he had been weeping abundantly.

Now it happened that the king, who had grown old, felt his strength diminishing. He called together his court and his family, and made his last wishes known to them. When he had done so, he kept no one with him but his most faithful servant.

"As soon as I am dead," he said, "I want you to take this key hanging around my neck on a golden chain. And to open the door of the secret room. But beforehand you must have procured a sack, and tied a blindfold over your eyes. As you go into the room with outstretched arms, you will find a portrait. Without removing your blindfold, you are to put this portrait in the sack. Then you must go to the great jetty in the port and throw the sack and its contents into the waves. Thus this portrait, which for half a century has been the source of both the joy and the sorrow in my life, will cease to exert its power, which on the whole is pernicious."

Whereupon he closed his eyes and expired.

The faithful servant scrupulously executed the king's orders. He took the key to the secret room, procured a sack, blindfolded his eyes, opened the door of the room, took the portrait, put it in the sack without looking at it, and threw the whole into the sea.

A short time afterward, however, it happened that a poor fisherman named Antar, having caught a shark, did not fail to cut open its stomach, for these most voracious of all fish sometimes have pleasant surprises in store for those who catch them. And its stomach contained the sack in which the portrait was imprisoned. When he got home, Antar thus discovered the face of a blond woman, and this face was so beautiful that the fisherman immediately knew, with both terror and rapture, that from then on nothing else in the whole world would be of interest in his eyes. Thus this painted visage, after having been the source of the king's joy and sorrow, both fulfilled and devastated the life of the humblest of his subjects.

Antar neglected his boat and his nets for three days, and when, on the entreaties of his wife and children, he brought himself to go back to sea, he came back in the evening emptyhanded. He came back empty-handed, his family would go hungry, but a strange smile, at once sad and ecstatic, played over his lips—the smile of the lovers of the blond queen.

Now, the eldest son of this fisherman was twelve years old, and his first name was Riad. This child had proved so gifted for the sciences of the mind and the arts of the soul that the sage, poet, and calligrapher Ibn Al Houdaïda had taken him under his protection, in order to communicate his knowledge to him. When his master questioned him about his haggard mien, Riad did not hesitate to recount the misfortune that had struck his father and the strange state of languor into which he had fallen.

"And that blond queen," the sage asked him, "have you seen her yourself?"

"Oh no!" cried the child. "My father hides her, and guards her with fierce jealousy. And besides, why should I want to see her?"

"That is just as it should be, at least for the present," said the sage with approval. "But when you are a little more seasoned, you will certainly have to risk looking at her—if, that is, you really want to rescue your father from an evil spell."

"And how shall I go about it?"

"It is a question of an image; that is to say, a set of lines deeply embedded in the flesh so as to cause anyone who falls under their ascendancy to become enslaved to matter," Ibn Al Houdaïda replied. "The image is endowed with the power to paralyze, as for instance the head of Medusa, which turned to stone all those who came within its gaze. Yet this fascination is only irresistible to the eyes of the illiterate. Indeed, the image is no more than a jumble of signs, and its maleficent force comes from the confused, discordant sum of their meanings, as the fall and clash of milliards of drops of sea water together create the lugubrious howling of the storm, instead of the crystalline harmony that an ear endowed with superhuman discernment would be capable of hearing. For the literate man, the image is not mute. Its wild-beast roar unravels into many mellifluous words. It is only a question of being able to read . . ."

Riad at once began to learn to read. His master taught him first that *figure* does not only refer to the human face and form, but that there are also figures of rhetoric. These include *figures of diction* (in which the form of words is modified), such as prothesis, epenthesis, paragoge, aphaeresis, syncope, apocope, metathesis, diaeresis, synthesis, and crasis. They are also *figures of construction* (which concern the natural order of words), such as ellipsis, zeugma, syllepsis, hyperbaton, and pleonasm. And *figures of speech,* or *tropes,* such as metaphor, irony, allegory, allusion, catachresis, hypallage, synecdoche, metonymy, euphemism, antonomasia, metalepsis, and antiphrasis. And finally, *figures of thought,* such as antithesis, apostrophe, epiphenomenon, subjection, obsecration, hyperbole, litotes, prosopopoeia, and hypotyposis.

And these thirty-six figures already formed a throng, but they were merely some of the infinite number of figures that surrounded him wherever he went, just as over certain icons a swarm of cherubs' winged faces may be seen accompanying the labors and the days of a saint.

But this was still only literature, and the master placed the slit, beveled reed pen in his hand, and with it he learned to trace in mulberry juice on a sheet of parchment the twenty-eight letters of the alphabet (twenty-nine, if we regard lam-alif as an extra letter).

From this day on, the adolescent advanced through the dangerous world of images armed with his reed pen and calligraphic signs, as a young hunter plunges into a dark forest with his bow and arrows. But the image his master taught him to beware of more than any other was the human face, because for the illiterate it is the most vivid source of fear, of shame, and above all of hate and love.

He told him:

"There is one infallible sign by which one can tell if one is truly in love with someone. This is when her face inspires us with more physical desire than any other part of her body."

He also said:

"One of the secrets of the power of the face lies in its specular form. For it seems to be composed of two identical halves separated by the median line that passes through the middle of the forehead, the bridge of the nose, and the point of the chin. But this symmetry is only superficial. For anyone who knows how to read the signs of which it is formed, it should rather be seen as two poems full of assonances and resonances, but whose echo reverberates all the more loudly in that, in spite of their affinity, they do not mean the same thing."

He took from his coffer the portrait of a bearded man with a grave, imperious expression that radiated a will to subjugate, regardless, everything and everyone he found in his path.

"What does this face inspire in you?" he asked Riad.

"Respectful fear," the boy replied. "And also a kind of pity. You would want to obey him, but only because you were afraid. If it were possible, you would also want to be able to like him a little."

"That is very well seen. This portrait is of Sultan Omar, the whole of whose reign was nothing but a series of violent and treacherous acts. But since you are now literate, and therefore capable of it, it is essential that you liberate yourself from the obscure rays emanating from this portrait. Observe carefully what I do."

He picked up a reed pen and traced the following words in broad calligraphic characters on the right-hand side of the parchment:

The Child is father of the Man [1]

Then he chose another sheet and, in a winged hand, he wrote on its left-hand side:

Young wounds, great destinies [2]

On the right-hand side of a third parchment, he wrote next:

Beware of the dreams of youth; they always end by coming true [3]

Note: These eternal truths, written in the lines of the face, have been expressed many times over the centuries and the millennia. We have chosen to take them from the following writers:
[1] William Wordsworth.
[2], [7], [11] Ibn Al Houdaïda.
[3] Goethe.
[4] Alain.
[5] Paul Valéry.
[6] Germaine de Staël.
[8], [9], [10], [12], [13] Edward Reinroth.

Then, on the left-hand side of another sheet, he wrote:

Power drives men mad,
absolute power drives them absolutely mad[4]

Finally, on a last sheet, he wrote these words, but this time over the whole surface of the sheet:

A man alone is always in bad company[5]

"And now—look carefully!"

Riad's eyes were wide with amazement as he watched Ibn Al Houdaïda superimpose the five translucent parchments covered with calligraphic arabesques. For what appeared in filigree, as if on the bottom of a tranquil lake, was a face, the face of Sultan Omar, with its bitter, brutal expression, but nevertheless also tempered by the wounded tenderness that had struck Riad.

"And that is not all," the wise calligrapher continued. "Observe this too."

He changed the order in which the parchment sheets had been superimposed—once, twice, thrice—and each time the sultan's expression changed subtly, and its dominant aspect became now imperious will, now cruelty, now the memory of a childhood deprived of tenderness.

"It's inevitable," the master explained. "The top sheet can be seen much more clearly than the bottom one. The three others also show through to a certain extent. But isn't that what happens in life?"

"True," Riad agreed, "there are several men in each one of us, and it is now one, now the other, that animates our face."

"And this face is nothing other than an aggregate of signs expressing an intelligible truth," Ibn Al Houdaïda concluded, "but we only perceive it approximatively, as a cry, a threat, or a sob. And now—go! Go and confront the painted queen, and save your father from her ascendancy. Take your ink, your parchments, and your pens, and go home."

Riad darted off toward the family house.

The boat had been hauled up onto the shore, and it was clear that it had not been to sea for several days. The wide-open house door revealed the wretchedness of his mother and her children. But Riad knew that everything was taking place in the ramshackle wooden shed in which Antar stored his nets and tackle, and which he kept jealously locked. This hut had in fact become the temple of the blond queen, and the boy had to muster up all his courage to go and knock on its door. There was no answer. The door was bolted, but worm-eaten, and with only slight pressure from his shoulder Riad was able to force his way into the hut. A candle flame pierced the darkness, like the dim light burning in a chapel. In its faint, flickering glow, all that could be seen was a face; the face of the blond queen.

Riad moved forward in the darkness, irresistibly attracted by the portrait. It was the first time he had seen it, and its maleficent power made a deep impression on the pure youth. He fell on his knees as if before an idol, and it seemed to him that he was being drawn helplessly into the depths of that white face, that golden hair, those blue eyes.

Minutes passed. Riad grew accustomed to the dim light, and some details of the interior of the hut began to appear; broken oars, tangled fishing lines, baskets and wicker lobster pots full of holes, a whole tragic disorder that spoke of the shipwreck of a profession, but over which hovered the enigmatic smile of the queen.

But then Riad noticed his parchments, his ink, and his reed pens at his feet, this modest schoolboy equipment that was to arm him against the fascination of the image. So he sat down cross-legged, put his writing book on his knees, took a pen in his right hand, and observed the portrait with an eye cleansed and revived by studious attention.

He did not have to look long before he saw that this face—like that of every living being, no doubt—was not exactly symmetrical. He first considered the left eye, which clearly did not say the same thing as the right eye. What was it saying, that left eye? With a skilled hand, Riad traced the main lines of which it was composed, and these lines said:

Glory is the dazzling mourning of happiness[6]

Then on another sheet he copied the right eye, and found he had written these words:

The eye of a queen must know how to be blind[7]

Next it was the turn of the straight little nose to be traced, its line very slightly upturned in subdued insolence. Then he deciphered these words:

Smell is the opposite of scent[8]

He had thus deciphered the three median lines of the human face. There remained, above, the forehead. And the line of the forehead meant:

The honor of a queen is a snow-covered field without trace of footsteps[9]

Finally, below, the firm, willful contour of the chin said:

That which woman desires, man believes he wants[10]

There remained only the most disturbing, the most difficult part of the portrait, the mass of blond hair kept in check by the crown, but escaping it in two impetuous streams. Riad covered a whole sheet of parchment with intermingled signs, in such a way that an ignorant man would have seen nothing but a skein of soft, silky hair. But for one who knew how to read, the right-hand side of this skein said:

Blond is innocence[11]

And the left-hand side:

Fair hair, light woman[12]

To complete his work, Riad drew the smooth, regular velvet material surmounting the metallic circle of the crown. And

that golden hair, enclosed in a golden circle, perfectly arranged and disciplined, said:

Justice, fidelity, pure heart[13]

"Wretch! What are you doing there?"

Antar's dark silhouette was outlined in the bright rectangle
of the doorway. Riad stood up, trembling. The fisherman had
seized a harpoon and was preparing to hurl it at this intruder,
whom he could not recognize in the shadows.

"Stop, Father, it's Riad, your son!"

"Who gave you permission to force the door and come in
here?"

His tone was still menacing, but the harpoon was already
slanting toward the ground.

"My master has taught me a new way to pay homage to the
painted queen."

"This image belongs to me alone. I forbid you to look at it!"

"I no longer need to look at it. I have something much
better now," Riad explained, showing his father the parchment sheets he was holding.

"What does that mean?"

That was the whole question. That was the great question
Riad had been waiting for. He went to the door and placed
himself in the light.

"Exactly, Father. I came with my reed pens, my ink, and my
parchments to decipher the meaning of the blond queen. And
this is what I found."

He held up to the sky the eight superimposed sheets he had
covered with calligraphic signs. Immediately the face of the
queen appeared, a face composed of arabesques, a translucent,
appeased, spiritualized face.

Antar dropped his harpoon and seized the sheets, the better
to examine them. He was subjugated by this divine version of
the portrait which for so long had brutally enslaved him.

"I don't understand," he murmured.

"You don't understand everything," Riad explained, "because you can only read a few letters. But you can see that these pen strokes recite a poem, the lament of the blond queen who is the victim of her own beauty."

And in his clear adolescent voice, he sang the melancholy song of a child doomed to be haplessly loved because of her infamous origins, who became a dangerously desirable girl, and then a woman hated by some, adored by others, and finally achieved a kind of peace only through the austere and solitary exercise of power.

He spoke, he went on speaking, his father's eyes went from his lips to the parchment sheets, and the fisherman strove to repeat each word, each phrase, as one learns a prayer, an incantation designed to exorcise a magic spell.

The next day Riad returned to his master to continue his studies. And Antar went back to sea. But every evening, father and son went to the hut and, under the enigmatic but henceforth harmless smile of the blond queen, the adolescent initiated his father into the great art and profound wisdom of calligraphy.

Twenty-seven

ACHOUR WAS JUBILANT.

"Place Vendôme! Ah, my cousin! It's the ultra chic of Paris high life. Jewelers, perfumeries, the Ritz Hotel, and the Ministry of Justice. And over and above it all, the great Napoleon on his column! No, your imagination can't take all that in. And us wogs, what are we doing there? We come along with our tools, and we smash it all up!"

They were going to start digging a four-level underground car park capable of engulfing up to nine hundred cars. Work that would last for several months, and in the most elegant part of Paris. Unmoved by this detail, Idris was more interested in the tool he was going to have to handle, a pneumatic drill, which was new to him but had become almost the symbol of the Maghrebi worker.

The men were already in the square at daybreak, white-helmeted, leather-gloved, with the first trucks and the trailer carrying the compressor. The public works department were already putting up their asbestos-cement huts.

Idris wandered off, sniffing out the land. Achour hadn't lied.

Everything here radiated chic, money, and La Vieille France. On one side, the Ritz and the lofty façade of the former chancellery. On the other, shopwindows whose very sobriety spelled sumptuousness, opulence, luxury. One after the other he deciphered trade names whose prestige meant nothing to him: Guerlain, Morabito, Houbigant, Bank of India, Boucheron, Schiaparelli, les must de Cartier, Les Bois du Gabon. He stopped in front of a jeweler's. Protected by a tinted-glass window as thick as one's thumb and fortified with vibration sensors, a river of diamonds sparkled against a cushion of garnet-red silk. The little shepherd from Tabelbala felt the full force of the kind of arrogance radiating from the splendid jewel. He went back to his workmates, who were standing around the engineer, the architect, and the foreman. Brief remarks were being exchanged.

"The entry to the car park, Rue de Castiglione side. The exit, Rue de la Paix side."

"Aren't you afraid the Colonne Vendôme will collapse?"

"Given its weight, it won't budge. But if the façades of the buildings were to crack we'd look silly!"

In the meantime, the diesel engine in the compressor was beginning to hiccup. The umbilical cord joining it to the drill was writhing on the little paving stones in the square. Achour had taken the drill and was giving Idris a lesson.

"You see, my cousin, this is the way you hold it. Don't let your stomach touch it, it'd give you the colic."

One of the workers broke in vehemently:

"Yes, you've got to watch out. Those are the filthiest things they ever invented to kill Arabs with! If you don't watch out, your hair gets blown off, you swallow your teeth, and your stomach goes crashing down into your boots!"

Achour protested:

"No, no, it's not that bad! A pneumatic drill's great, believe me. It's your prick, don't you see? A giant prick. With that thing you can stuff Paris, you can screw France!"

Everyone around him laughed. Idris had got hold of the

hand grips. The body of the drill, with its exhaust ports and its springs, amounted to twenty-five kilos of steel oscillating above the drill bit, the working shaft that terminated in a broad cold chisel. There was a rectangle of loose ground on which Idris could try it out. He pressed down the throttle lever. Immediately, volleys of compressed air were let off in frantic succession. Idris realized the indispensable role played by the operator's bones and muscles at one of the extremities of the tool. At the other extremity, the chisel wouldn't be able to do its work of destruction and penetration without the support of this living, resilient cushion. When the bit had penetrated thirty centimeters into the ground, Idris cut off the air intake and tried to pull the tool out. This was what the watching workers had been waiting for and joking about: the bit remained firmly stuck in the solid earth. He should have rotated the drill to crack the crust of the ground before sinking it in so deeply.

"Start it up again and pull it toward you," Achour advised him.

The pyrotechnics resumed, and Idris leaned backward and braced himself. But it was now his whole body, and chiefly the small of his back, that took the full force of each impact. He stopped, dazed by the blows, like a boxer who has just been on the receiving end of a series of jabs to the stomach.

Meanwhile, the foreman had drawn a series of chalk lines on the pavement to indicate the direction of the first trench to be dug. Idris went over to it, dragging the cable of his drill.

CRISTOBAL AND CO.
Jewels & Gems
From Africa and the Middle East

Idris read these letters on the nearest shopwindow. One single jewel was displayed in it: the golden droplet shone in solitary splendor on a black velvet cushion. Idris couldn't believe his eyes: it was there, beyond all doubt, the *bulla aurea*, seen for the first time around Zett Zobeida's neck, lost in the hot Marseille street, oval, slightly swollen at its base, of so admirable a shape and brilliance that it seemed to create a void around it, the symbol of freedom, the antidote to enslavement by the image. It was there, hanging behind that simple shopwindow, and Idris, as he looked at it, leaned on his formidable instrument designed to demolish the asphalt. He had forgotten his workmates, the foreman who was becoming impatient, the Place Vendôme with its emperor on his column. Once again he saw Zett Zobeida dancing in the night with her jingling jewelry, with her silent golden droplet. He put the tip of his drill down on the macadam and pressed the lever. The ferruginous thunder pervaded his whole body. But this time a tappet that had suddenly worked loose and gone mad accompanied the machine-gun fire with a strident, metallic tintinnabulation. It was a frenzied jangle, a sound of high-pitched castanets, an infernal sleigh bell. The asphalt crust came up easily, like a snakeskin. Idris moved up and down without switching off his drill. It was his dancing partner, Zett Zobeida metamorphosed into a rabid robot.

DANCING ON THE SPOT with his pneumatic drill, he didn't notice the Cristobal & Co. window crack from top to bottom. He didn't hear the wail of the alarm bell triggered off by the vibration sensors. Ding, ding, ding. Idris was still dancing, his head full of a phantasmagoria of dragonflies, crickets, and jewels all jumping up and down in delirious frenzy. A police van blocked off the Rue de Castiglione. Another stationed itself across the Rue de la Paix. Helmeted policemen in bulletproof vests poured out of them and ran up to the window starred with cracks which went on howling like a wounded animal. Deaf and blind, Idris went on dancing in front of the golden droplet with his pneumatic dancing partner.

POSTSCRIPT

FOR PARISIANS, the Rue de la Goutte-d'Or ("Street of the Golden Droplet") in the XVIIIth arrondissement has symbolic value. It is the center of the district where African immigrant workers congregate, and it was the scene of violent clashes during the Algerian War. But its name needs some explanation.

In former days, the Montmartre hill was entirely covered with vineyards, and those of the Barbès district produced a well-known white wine, from which the street took its name. But it already has a literary history. It is over a hundred years since Zola published his novel on alcoholism, *L'Assommoir;* its title refers to the tavern Zola situated in the Rue de la Goutte-d'Or.

One reason why I called this book *La Goutte d'or* is of course the fact that its hero is an African immigrant worker. But the title has other connotations. The golden droplet in this novel is also a geometrically shaped Berber jewel. It symbolizes abstract, nonfigurative beauty; in short, the preeminence of the sign over the image. Other Berber jewels portray flowers, dogs, insects, etc., but the golden droplet represents nothing; it is a pure sign. The ancient Romans gave their freeborn children a golden bubble *(bulla aurea)* to wear, as a symbol both of their childish innocence and of their status as freeborn men. When the Roman adolescent exchanged his child's toga *(praetexta)* for the virile toga *(virilis)*, he also abandoned his *bulla aurea*. It is this loss of both his innocence and his freedom that Idris, the young Berber who has come to Paris, experiences in the course of the episodes of this novel.

THE SAHARA is far more than the Sahara. Islam is a bottomless well. My many journeys to the Maghreb and the Near East have above all allowed me to measure my own ignorance. I can only mention a few names among all those who have helped me write this book:

Dominique Champault, who is the head of the Department of White Africa in the Musée de l'Homme, and whose book *Tabelbala*[1] is a model of what the ethnological monograph should be, and an inexhaustible source of information.

Salah Riza, who not only has written *L'Hégire des exclus*[2] but was my guide in the hostels for Maghrebi workers in the Paris region.

El Gherbi, who revealed Marseille to me—African Marseille.

And all those who, more erudite than I, have been good enough to answer my questions: Germaine Tillion, Roger Frison-Roche, Leila Menchari, Claude Blanguernon, Marcel Ichac, and Ysabel Saïah, who knows everything about Oum Kalsoum.[3]

I would particularly like to pay homage to the memory of Colonel Alexandre Bernard. I met him shortly before his death, near Bourg-en-Bresse, on the farm to which he had

[1] Published by Centre National de la Recherche Scientifique.
[2] Published by Ken Productions.
[3] Her book *Oum Kalsoum* was published by Denoël.

retired. In 1920 he was twenty-six, and it was he who piloted General Laperrine's plane. The evocation of Sigisbert de Beaufond—an invented character, and a mythomaniac into the bargain, since he identifies himself with Alexandre Bernard—is based on Bernard's own account, a recording of which I still have. As a result, all the details reported are authentic—even down to Laperrine's temporary grave dug in the furrow made by the plane and surmounted by one of its wheels, itself crowned by the general's kepi. When Sigisbert de Beaufond holds out his wrists to show the scars of his attempted suicide, obviously Idris can't see anything. But I did see those scars on Bernard's wrists.

Finally, I would like to thank the master calligrapher Hassan Massoudy, who enabled me to approach a traditional art whose beauty is indistinguishable from truth and wisdom.[4]

M.T.

[4] His *Calligraphie arabe vivante* was published by Flammarion.